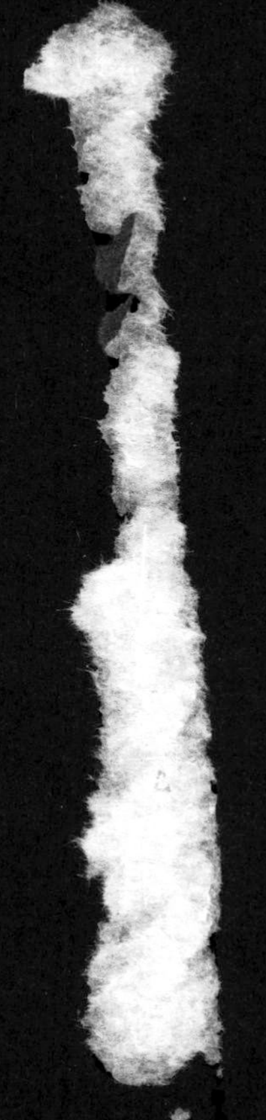

THE SHAPE OF WATER

ANDREA CAMILLERI

THE SHAPE OF WATER

Translated by Stephen Sartarelli

PICADOR

First published 2002 by Viking Penguin,
a member of Penguin Putnam Inc., New York

First published in Great Britain 2003 by Picador
an imprint of Pan Macmillan Ltd
Pan Macmillan, 20 New Wharf Road, London N1 9RR
Basingstoke and Oxford
Associated companies throughout the world
www.panmacmillan.com

ISBN 0 330 49289 6 HB

Originally published in Italian as *La forma dell'acqua* by Sellerio Editore, Palermo.

1 3 5 7 9 8 6 4 2

A CIP catalogue record for this book is available from
the British Library.

Typeset by Intype London Ltd
Printed and bound in Great Britain by
Mackays of Chatham plc, Chatham, Kent

THE SHAPE OF WATER

ONE

No light of daybreak filtered yet into the courtyard of Splendour, the company under government contract to collect trash in the town of Vigàta. A low, dense mass of clouds completely covered the sky as though a great grey tarpaulin had been drawn from one corner to another. Not a single leaf fluttered. The sirocco was late to rise from its leaden sleep, yet people already struggled to exchange a few words. The foreman, before assigning the areas to be cleaned, announced that this day, and for some days to come, Peppe Schèmmari and Caluzzo Brucculeri would be absent, excused from work. More than excused, they'd been arrested: the previous evening they'd attempted to rob a supermarket, weapons in hand. To Pino Catalane and Saro Montaperto – young land surveyors naturally without employment as land surveyors, but hired by

Splendour as temporary 'ecological agents' thanks to the generous string-pulling of Chamber Deputy Cusumano, in whose electoral campaign the two had fought body and soul (and in that order, with the body doing far more than the soul felt like doing) – the foreman assigned the jobs vacated by Peppe and Caluzzo, that is, the sector that went by the name of the 'Pasture,' because in a time now beyond memory a goatherd had apparently let his goats roam there. It was a broad tract of Mediterranean brush on the outskirts of town that stretched almost as far as the shore. Behind it lay the ruins of a large chemical works inaugurated by the ubiquitous Deputy Cusumano when it seemed the magnificent winds of progress were blowing strong. Soon, however, that breeze changed into the flimsiest of puffs before dropping altogether, but in that brief time it had managed to do more damage than a tornado, leaving a shambles of compensation benefits and unemployment in its wake. To prevent the crowds of black and not-so-black Senegalese, Algerians, Tunisians and Libyans wandering about the city from nesting in that factory, a high wall had been built all around it, above which the old structures still soared, corroded by weather, neglect and sea salt, looking more and more like architectures designed by Gaudi under the influence of hallucinogens.

Until recently the Pasture had represented, for those who at the time still went under the undignified name of garbage collectors, a cakewalk of a job: amid the scraps of paper, plastic bags, cans of beer and Coca-Cola, and shit piles barely covered up or left out in the open air, now and then a used condom would appear, and it would set one thinking, provided one had the desire and imagination to do so, about the details of that encounter. For a good year now, however, the occasional condom had turned into an ocean, a carpet of condoms, ever since a certain minister with a dark, taciturn face worthy of a Lombroso diagram had fished deep into his mind, which was even darker and more mysterious than his face, and come up with an idea he thought would solve all the south's law and order problems. He had managed to sell this idea to a colleague of his who dealt with the army and who, for his part, looked as if he had walked right out of a Pinocchio illustration, and together the two had decided to send a number of detachments to Sicily for the purpose of 'controlling the territory', to lighten the load of the carabinieri, local police, intelligence services, special operations teams, coastguard, the highway police, railway police and port police, the anti-Mafia, anti-terrorism, anti-drug, anti-theft and anti-kidnapping commissions, and others – here omitted for the sake of brevity – quite busy with other business. Thanks to the brilliant idea of these two eminent statesmen, all the Piedmontese mama's boys and beardless Friulian conscripts who just the night before had enjoyed the crisp, fresh air of their mountains suddenly found themselves painfully short of breath, huffing in their temporary lodgings, in towns that stood barely a yard above sea level, among people who spoke an incomprehensible dialect consisting not so much of words as of silences, indecipherable movements of the eyebrows, imperceptible puckerings of the facial wrinkles. They adapted as best they could, thanks to their young age, and were given a helping hand by the residents of Vigàta themselves, who were moved to pity by the foreign boys' lost, bewildered looks. The one who saw to lessening the hardship of their exile was a certain Gegè Gullotta, a fast thinker who until that moment had been forced to suppress his natural gifts as a pimp by dealing in light drugs. Having learned through channels both underhanded and ministerial of the soldiers' imminent arrival, Gegè had had a flash of genius, and to put said flash to work for him he had promptly appealed to the beneficence of those in charge of such matters in order to obtain all the countless convoluted authorizations indispensable to his plan – those in charge being, that is, those who truly controlled the area and would never have dreamt of issuing officially stamped permits. Gegè, in short, succeeded in opening a specialized market of fresh meat and many and sundry drugs, all light, at the Pasture. Most of the meat came from the former Eastern Bloc countries, now free at last of the communist yoke which, as everyone knows, had denied all personal, human dignity; now, between the Pasture's bushes and sandy shore, come nightfall, that reconquered dignity shone again in all its magnificence. But there was also no lack of Third World women, transvestites, transsexuals, Neapolitan faggots, Brazilian *viados* – something for every taste, a feast, an embarrassment of riches. And business flourished, to the great satisfaction of the soldiers, Gegè and those who, for a proper cut of the proceeds, had granted Gegè permission to operate.

Pino and Saro headed toward their assigned work

sector, each pushing his own cart. To get to the Pasture took half an hour, if one was slow of foot as they were. The first fifteen minutes they spent without speaking, already sweaty and sticky. It was Saro who broke the silence.

'That Pecorilla is a bastard,' he announced.

'A fucking bastard,' clarified Pino.

Pecorilla was the foreman in charge of assigning the areas to be cleaned, and he nurtured an undisguised hatred for anyone with an education, having himself managed to finish middle school, at age forty, only thanks to Cusumano, who had a man to man talk with the teacher. Thus he manipulated things so that the hardest, most demeaning work always fell to the three university graduates in his charge. That same morning, in fact, he had assigned to Ciccu Loreto the stretch of wharf from which the mail boat sailed for the island of Lampedusa. Which meant that Ciccu, with his accounting degree, would be forced to account for the piles of trash that noisy mobs of tourists, many-tongued yet all sharing the same utter disregard for personal and public cleanliness, had left behind on Saturday and Sunday while waiting to embark. And no doubt Pino and Saro, after the soldiers' two days off duty, would find the Pasture one big glory hole.

When they reached the corner of Via Lincoln and Viale Kennedy (in Vigàta there was even a Cortile Eisenhower and a Vicolo Roosevelt), Saro stopped.

'I'm going to run upstairs and see how the little guy's doing,' he said to his friend. 'Wait here. I'll only be a minute.'

Without waiting for Pino's answer, he slipped into one of those midget high-rises that were not more than twelve storeys high, having been built around the same time as the chemical works and having just as quickly fallen into ruin, when not abandoned altogether. For someone approaching from the sea, Vigàta rose up like a parody of Manhattan, on a reduced scale. And this explained, perhaps, the names of some of its streets.

Nenè, the little guy, was awake; he slept on and off for some two hours a night, spending the rest of the time with eyes wide open, without ever crying. Who had ever seen a baby that didn't cry? Day after day he was consumed by an illness of unknown cause and cure. The doctors of Vigàta couldn't figure it out; his parents would have to take him somewhere else, to some big-shot specialist, but they didn't have the money. Nenè grew sullen as soon as his eyes met his father's, a wrinkle forming across his forehead. He couldn't talk, but had expressed himself quite clearly with that silent reproach of the person who had put him in these straits. 'He's doing a little better, the fever's going down,' said Tana, Saro's wife, just to make him happy.

*

The clouds had scattered, and now the sun was blazing hot enough to shatter rocks. Saro had already emptied his cart a dozen times in the garbage bin that had appeared, thanks to private initiative, where the rear exit of the factory used to be, and his back felt broken. When he was a few steps from the path that ran along the enclosure wall and led to the provincial road, he saw something sparkle violently on the ground. He bent down to have a better look. It was a heart-shaped pendant, enormous, studded with little diamonds all around and with one great big diamond in the middle. The solid-gold chain was still attached, though broken in one spot. Saro's right hand shot out, grabbed the necklace, and stuffed it in his pocket. The hand seemed to have acted on its own, before his brain, still flabbergasted by the discovery, could tell it anything. Standing up again, drenched in sweat, he looked around but didn't see a living soul.

*

Pino, who had chosen to work the stretch of the Pasture nearest the beach, at one point spotted the nose of a car about twenty yards away, sticking out of some bushes a bit denser than the rest. Unsure, he stopped; it wasn't possible someone could still be around here at this hour, seven in the morning, screwing a whore. He began to approach cautiously, one step at a time, almost bent over, and when he'd reached the taillights he quickly stood straight up. Nothing happened, nobody shouted to fuck off, the car seemed vacant. Coming nearer, he finally made out the indistinct shape of a man, motionless, in the passenger seat, head thrown back. He seemed to be in a deep sleep. But by the look and the smell of it, Pino realized something was fishy. He turned around and called to Saro, who came running, out of breath, eyes bulging. 'What is it? What the hell do you want?' Pino thought his friend's questions a bit aggressive but blamed it on the fact that he had run all that way. 'Get a load of this,' he said.

Plucking up his courage, Pino went up to the driver's side and tried to open the door but couldn't: it was locked. With the help of Saro, who seemed to have calmed down, he tried to reach the other door, against which the man's body was partially leaning, but the car, a large green BMW , was too close to the shrub to allow anyone to approach from that side. Leaning forward, however, and getting scratched by the brambles, they managed to get a better look at the man's face. He was not sleeping; his eyes were wide open and motionless. The moment they realized that the man was dead, Pino and Saro froze in terror – not at the sight of death but because they recognized him.

*

'I feel like I'm taking a sauna,' said Saro as he ran along the provincial road toward a telephone booth. 'A blast of cold one minute, a blast of heat the next.'

They had agreed on one thing since overcoming their paralysis upon recognizing the deceased: before alerting the police, they had to make another phone call. They knew Deputy Cusumano's number by heart, and Saro dialled it. But Pino didn't let the phone ring even once.

'Hang up, quick!' he said.

Saro obeyed automatically.

'You don't want to tell him?'

'Let's just think for a minute, let's think hard. This is very important. You know as well as I do that Cusumano is a puppet.'

'What's that supposed to mean?'

'He's a puppet of Luparello, who is everything – or was everything. With Luparello dead, Cusumano's a nobody, a doormat.'

'So?'

'So nothing.'

They turned back toward Vigàta, but after a few steps Pino stopped Saro.

'Rizzo, the lawyer,' he said.

'I'm not going to call that guy. He gives me the creeps. I don't even know him.'

'I don't either, but I'm going to call him anyway.'

Pino got the number from the operator. Though it was still only seven forty-five, Rizzo answered after the first ring.

'Mr Rizzo?'

'Yes?'

'Excuse me for bothering you at this hour, Mr Rizzo, but . . . we found Mr Luparello, you see, and . . . well, he looks dead.'

There was a pause. Then Rizzo spoke.

'So why are you telling me this?'

Pino was stunned. He was ready for anything, except that bizarre response.

'But . . . aren't you his best friend? We thought it was only right—'

'I appreciate it. But you must do your duty first. Good day.'

Saro had been listening to the conversation, his cheek pressed against Pino's. They looked at each other, nonplussed. Rizzo acted as if they'd told him they'd just found some nameless cadaver.

'Shit! He was his friend, wasn't he?' Saro burst out.

'What do we know? Maybe they had a fight,' said Pino to reassure him.

'So what do we do now?'

'We go and do our duty, like the lawyer said,' concluded Pino.

They headed toward town, to police headquarters. The thought of going to the carabinieri didn't even cross their minds, since they were under the command of a Milanese lieutenant. The Vigàta police inspector, on the other hand, was from Catania, a certain Salvo Montalbano, who, when he wanted to get to the bottom of something, he did.

TWO

'Again.'

'No,' said Livia, still staring at him, her eyes more luminous from the amorous tension.

'Please.'

'No, I said no.'

I always like being forced a little, he remembered her whispering once in his ear; and so, aroused, he tried slipping his knee between her closed thighs as he gripped her wrists roughly and spread her arms until she looked as though crucified.

They eyed each other a moment, panting, when suddenly she surrendered.

'Yes,' she said. 'Now.'

At that exact moment the phone rang. Without even opening his eyes, Montalbano reached out with his arm to grab not the telephone so much as the fluttering shreds of the dream now inexorably vanishing.

'Hello!' he shouted angrily at the intruder.

'Inspector, we've got a client.' He recognized Sergeant Fazio's voice; the other sergeant, Tortorella, was still in the hospital with the nasty bullet he'd taken in the belly from some would-be Mafioso who was actually just a pathetic two-bit jerk-off. In their jargon a 'client' meant a death they should look into.

'Who is it?'

'We don't know yet.'

'How was he killed?'

'We don't know. Actually, we don't even know if he was killed.'

'I don't get it, Sergeant. You woke me up to tell me you don't know a goddamn thing?'

Montalbano breathed deeply to dispel his pointless anger, which Fazio tolerated with the patience of a saint.

'Who found him?' he continued.

'A couple of garbage collectors in the Pasture. They found him in a car.'

'I'll be right there. Meanwhile phone the Montelusa department, have them send someone from the lab, and inform Judge Lo Bianco.'

*

As he stood under the shower, he reached the conclusion that the dead man must have been a member of the Cuffaro gang. Eight months earlier, probably due to some territorial dispute, a ferocious war had broken out between the Vigàta Cuffaros and the Sinagra gang, who were from Fela. One victim per month, by turns, and in orderly fashion: one in Vigàta, one in Fela. The latest, a certain Mario Salino, had been shot in Fela by the Vigatese, so now it was apparently the turn of one of the Cuffaro thugs.

Before going out – he lived alone in a small house right on the beach on the opposite side of town from the Pasture – he felt like calling Livia in Genoa. She answered immediately, drowsy with sleep.

'Sorry, but I wanted to hear your voice.'

'I was dreaming of you,' she said. 'You were here with me.'

Montalbano was about to say that he, too, had

been dreaming of her, but an absurd prudishness held him back. Instead he asked: 'And what were we doing?'

'Something we haven't done for too long,' she said.

*

At headquarters, aside from the sergeant, there were only three policemen. The rest had gone to the home of a clothing-shop owner who had shot his sister over a question of inheritance and then escaped. Montalbano opened the door to the interrogation room. The two garbage collectors were sitting on the bench, huddling one against the other, pale despite the heat.

'Wait here till I get back,' Montalbano said to them, and the two, resigned, didn't even reply. They both knew well that any time one fell in with the law, whatever the reason, it was going to be a long affair.

'Have any of you called the papers?' the inspector asked his men. They shook their heads no.

'Well, I don't want them sticking their noses in this. Make a note of that.'

Timidly, Galluzzo came forward, raising two fingers as if to ask if he could go to the bathroom.

'Not even my brother-in-law?'

Galluzzo's brother-in-law was a newsman with Televigàta who covered local crime, and Montalbano imagined the family squabbles that might break out if Galluzzo weren't to tell him anything. And Galluzzo was looking at him with pitiful, canine eyes.

'All right. But he should come only after the body's been removed. And no photographers.'

They set out in a squad car, leaving Giallombardo behind on duty. Gallo was at the wheel. Together with Galluzzo, he was often the butt of facile jokes, such as 'Hey, Inspector, what's new in the chicken coop?'

Knowing Gallo's driving habits, Montalbano admonished him, 'Don't speed. We're in no hurry.'

At the curve by the Carmelite church, Peppe Gallo could no longer restrain himself and accelerated, screeching the tyres as he rounded the bend. They heard a loud crack, like a pistol shot, and the car skidded to a halt. They got out. The right rear tyre hung flabbily, blown out. It had been well worked over by a sharp blade; the cuts were quite visible.

'Goddamn sons of bitches!' bellowed the sergeant.

Montalbano got angry in earnest.

'But you all know they cut our tyres twice a month! Jesus! And every morning I remind you: don't forget to check them before going out! But you arseholes don't give a shit! And you won't until the day somebody breaks his neck!'

For one reason or another, it took a good ten minutes to change the tyre, and when they got to the Pasture, the Montelusa crime lab team was already there. They were in what Montalbano called the meditative stage, that is, five or six agents circling round and round the spot where the car stood, hands usually in their pockets or behind their backs. They looked like philosophers absorbed in deep thought, but in fact their eyes were combing the ground for clues, traces, footprints. As soon as Jacomuzzi, head of the crime lab, saw Montalbano, he came running up.

'How come there aren't any newsmen?'

'I didn't want any.'

'Well, this time they're going to accuse you of trying to cover up a big story.' He was clearly upset. 'Do you know who the dead man is?'

'No. Who?'

'None other than the engineer, Silvio Luparello.'

'Shit!' was Montalbano's only comment.

'And do you know how he died?'

'No. And I don't want to know. I'll have a look at him myself.'

Offended, Jacomuzzi went back to his men. The lab photographer had finished, and now it was Dr Pasquano's turn. Montalbano noticed that the coroner was forced to work in an uncomfortable position, his body half inside the car, wiggling his way toward the passenger seat, where a dark silhouette could be seen. Fazio and the Vigàta officers were giving a hand to their Montelusa colleagues. The inspector lit a cigarette and turned to look at the chemical factory. That ruin fascinated him. He decided he would come back one day to take a few snapshots, which he'd send to Livia to explain some things about himself and his island that she was still unable to understand.

Lo Bianco's car pulled up and the judge stepped out, looking agitated.

'Is it really Luparello?' he asked.

Apparently Jacomuzzi had wasted no time.

'So it seems.'

The judge joined the lab group and began speaking excitedly with Jacomuzzi and Dr Pasquano, who in the meantime had extracted a bottle of rubbing alcohol from his briefcase and was disinfecting his hands. After a good while, long enough for Montalbano to broil in the sun, the men from the lab got back in their cars and left. As he passed Montalbano, Jacomuzzi said nothing. Behind him, the inspector heard an ambulance siren wind down. It was his turn now. He'd have to do the talking and acting; there was no escape. He shook himself from the torpor in which he was stewing and walked toward the car with the dead man inside. Halfway there, the judge blocked his path.

'The body can be removed now. And considering poor Luparello's notoriety, the quicker we do it the better. In any case, keep me posted daily as to how the investigation develops.'

He paused a moment, and then, to make the words he'd just said a little less peremptory: 'Give me a ring when you think it's appropriate,' he added. Another pause. Then, 'During office hours, of course.'

He walked away. During office hours, not at home. At home, it was well known, Judge Lo Bianco was busy penning a stuffy, puffy book, *The Life and Exploits of Rinaldo and Antonio Lo Bianco, Masters of Jurisprudence at the University of Girgenti at the Time of King Martin the Younger (1402–1409)*. These Lo Biancos, he claimed, however nebulously, were his ancestors.

'How did he die?' Montalbano asked the doctor.

'See for yourself,' said the doctor, standing aside.

Montalbano stuck his head inside the car, which felt like an oven (more specifically, a crematorium), took his first look at the corpse, and immediately thought of the police commissioner.

He thought of the commissioner not because he was in the habit of turning his thoughts up the hierarchical ladder at the start of every investigation, but merely because some ten days earlier he had spoken with old Commissioner Burlando, who was a friend of his, about a book by Ariès, *Western Attitudes Toward Death,* which they had both read. The commissioner had argued that every death, even the most abject, was sacred. Montalbano had retorted, in all sincerity, that in no death, not even a pope's, could he see anything sacred whatsoever.

He wished the commissioner were there beside him now, to see what he saw. This Luparello had always been an elegant sort, extremely well groomed in every physical detail. Now, however, his tie was gone, his shirt rumpled, his glasses askew, his jacket collar incongruously half turned up, his socks sagging so flaccidly that they covered his loafers. But what most struck the inspector was the sight of the trousers pulled down around the man's knees, the white of the underwear showing inside the trousers, the shirt rolled up together with the undershirt halfway up his chest.

And the sex organ obscenely, horridly exposed, thick and hairy, in stark contrast with the meticulous care shown over the rest of his person.

'But how did he die?' he asked the doctor again, coming out of the car.

'Seems obvious, don't you think?' Pasquano replied rudely. 'You did know he'd had heart surgery,' he continued, 'performed by a famous London surgeon?'

'No, I did not. I saw him on TV last Wednesday, and he looked in perfect health to me.'

'He may have looked healthy, but he wasn't. You know, in politics they're all like dogs: the minute they realize you can't defend yourself, they attack. Apparently he had a double bypass in London. They say it was a difficult operation.'

'Who was his doctor in Montelusa?'

'My colleague Capuano. He was getting weekly check-ups. His health was very important to him – you know, always wanted to look fit.'

'You think I should talk to Capuano?'

'Absolutely unnecessary. It's plain as day what happened here. Poor Mr Luparello felt like having a good lay in the Pasture, maybe with some exotic foreign slut, and he had it, all right, and left his carcass behind.'

He noticed that Montalbano had a faraway look in his eyes.

'Not convinced?'

'No.'

'Why not?'

'I don't really know, to tell you the truth. Can you send me the results of the autopsy tomorrow?'

'Tomorrow?! Are you crazy? Before Luparello I've got that twenty-year-old girl who was raped in a shepherd's hut and found eaten by dogs ten days later, and then there's Fofò Greco, who had his tongue cut out and his balls cut off before they hung him from a tree to die, and then—'

Montalbano cut this macabre list short.

'Pasquano, let's get to the point. When can you get me the results?'

'Day after tomorrow, if, in the meantime, I don't have to run all over town looking at other corpses.'

They said goodbye. Montalbano called over the sergeant and his men and told them what they had to do and when to load the body into the ambulance. He had Gallo drive him back to headquarters.

'You can go back afterwards and pick up the others. And if you speed, I'll break your neck.'

*

Pino and Saro signed the sworn statement. In it their every movement before and after they discovered the body was described. But it neglected to mention two important things which the garbage collectors had been careful not to reveal to the law. The first was that they had almost immediately recognized the dead man, the second that they had hastened to inform the lawyer Rizzo of their discovery. They headed back home, Pino apparently with his thoughts elsewhere, Saro now and again touching the pocket that still held the necklace.

Nothing would happen for at least another twenty-four hours. In the afternoon Montalbano went back to his house, threw himself down on the bed, and fell into a three-hour sleep. When he woke, as the mid-September sea was flat as a mirror, he went for a long swim. Back inside, he made himself a dish of spaghetti with a sauce of sea urchin pulp and turned on the television. Naturally, all the local news programmes were talking about Luparello's death. They sang his praises, and from time to time a politician would appear, with a face to fit the occasion, and enumerate the merits of the deceased and the problems created by his passing. But not a single one of them, not even the news programme of the opposition's channel, dared to mention where and in what circumstances the late lamented Luparello had met his end.

THREE

Saro and Tana had a bad night. There was no doubt Saro had discovered a secret treasure, the kind told about in tales where vagabond shepherds stumble upon ancient jars full of gold coins or find little lambs covered in diamonds. But here the matter was not at all as in olden times: the necklace, of modern construction, had been lost the day before, this much was certain, and by anyone's guess it was worth a fortune. Was it possible nobody had come forward to declare it missing? As they sat at their small kitchen table, with the television on and the window wide open, like every night, to keep the neighbours from getting nosy and gossiping at the sight of the slightest change, Tana wasted no time opposing her husband's intention to go and sell it that very day, as soon as the Siracusa brothers' jewellery shop reopened.

'First of all,' she said, 'we're honest people. We can't just go and sell something that's not ours.'

'But what are we supposed to do? You want me to go to the foreman and tell him I found a necklace, turn it over to him, and have him give it back to its owner when they come to reclaim it? That bastard Pecorilla'll sell it himself in ten seconds flat.'

'We could do something else. We could keep the necklace at home and in the meantime tell Pecorilla about it. Then if somebody comes for it, we'll give it to them.'

'What good will that do us?'

'There's supposed to be a percentage for people who find things like this. How much do you think it's worth?'

'Twenty million lire, easy,' Saro replied, immediately thinking he'd blurted out too high a figure. 'So let's say we get two million. Can you tell me how we're going to pay for all of Nenè's treatments with two million lire?'

They talked it over until dawn and only stopped because Saro had to go to work. But they'd reached a temporary agreement that allowed their honesty to remain intact: they would hang on to the necklace without whispering a word to anyone, let a week go by, and then, if nobody came forward, they'd pawn it.

When Saro, washed up and ready to leave, went to kiss his son, he had a surprise: Nenè was sleeping deeply, peacefully, as if he somehow knew that his father had found a way to make him well.

*

Pino couldn't sleep that night either. Speculative by nature, he liked the theatre and had acted in several well-meaning but increasingly rare amateur productions in and around Vigàta. So he read theatrical literature. As soon as his meagre earnings would allow him, he would rush off to Montelusa's only bookshop and buy his fill of comedies and dramas. He lived with his mother, who had a small pension, and getting food on the table was not really a problem. Over dinner his mother had made him tell her three times how he discovered the corpse, asking him each time to better explain a certain detail or circumstance. She'd done this so that she could retell the whole story the next day to her friends at church or at the market, proud to be privy to such knowledge and to have a son so clever as to get himself involved in such an important affair. Finally, around midnight, she'd gone to bed, and shortly thereafter Pino turned in as well. As for sleeping, however, there was no chance of that; something made him toss and turn under the sheets. He was speculative by nature, as we said, and thus, after wasting two hours trying to shut his eyes, he'd convinced himself it was no use, it might as well be Christmas Eve. He got up, washed his face, and went to sit at the little desk he had in his bedroom. He repeated to himself the story he had told his mother, and although every detail fitted and it all made sense, the buzz in his head was still there, in the background. It was like the 'hot-cold' guessing game: as long as he was reviewing everything he'd said, the buzz seemed to be saying, 'You're cold.' Thus the static must be coming from something he'd neglected to tell his mother. And in fact what he hadn't told her were the same things he, by agreement with Saro, had kept from Inspector Montalbano: their immediate recognition of the corpse and the phone call to Rizzo. And here the buzz became very loud and screamed, 'You're hot hot hot!' So he took a pen and paper and wrote down word for word the conversation he'd had with the lawyer. He reread it and made some corrections, forcing himself to remember even the pauses, which he wrote in, as in a theatrical script. When he had got it all down, he reread the final draft. Something in that dialogue still didn't work. But it was too late now; he had to go to Splendour.

*

Around ten o'clock in the morning, Montalbano's reading of the two Sicilian dailies, one from Palermo and the other from Catania, was interrupted by a phone call from the commissioner.

'I was told to send you thanks,' the commissioner began.

'Oh, really? On whose behalf?'

'On behalf of the bishop and our minister. Monsignor Teruzzi was pleased with the Christian charity – those were his exact words – which you, how shall I say, put into action by not allowing any unscrupulous, indecent journalists and photographers to paint and propagate lewd portraits of the deceased.'

'But I gave that order before I even knew who it was! I would have done the same for anybody.'

'I'm aware of that; Jacomuzzi told me everything. But why should I have revealed such an irrelevant detail to our holy prelate? Why should I disabuse him, or you, of your Christian charity? Such charity, my dear man, becomes all the more precious the loftier the position of the object of charity, you know what I mean? Just imagine, the bishop even quoted Pirandello.'

'No!'

'Oh, yes. He quoted *Six Characters in Search of an Author,* the line where the father says that one cannot be held forever to a less than honourable act, after a life of great integrity, just because of one moment of weakness. In other words, we cannot pass on to posterity the image of Luparello with his pants momentarily down.'

'What did the minister say?'

'He certainly didn't quote Pirandello, since he wouldn't even know who that is, but the idea, however tortuous and mumbled, was the same. And since he belongs to the same party as Luparello, he took the trouble to add another word.'

'What was that?'

'Prudence.'

'What's prudence got to do with this business?'

'I don't know, but that's the word he used.'

'Any news of the autopsy?'

'Not yet. Pasquano wanted to keep him in the fridge until tomorrow, but I talked him into examining him late this morning or early in the afternoon. I don't think we're going to learn anything new from that end, though.'

'No, probably not,' Montalbano concurred.

*

Returning to his newspapers, Montalbano learned much less from them than he already knew of the life, miracles, and recent death of Silvio Luparello, engineer. They merely served to refresh his memory. Heir to a dynasty of Montelusa builders (his grandfather had designed the old train station, his father the courthouse), young Silvio, after graduating with highest Honours from Milan Polytechnic, had returned to his hometown to carry on and expand the family business. A practising Catholic, he had embraced the political ideals of his grandfather, a passionate follower of Don Luigi Sturzo (the ideals of his father, who had been a Fascist militiaman and participated in the March on Rome, were kept under a respectful veil of silence), and had cut his teeth at the FUCI, the national organization of Catholic university students, creating a solid network of friendships for himself. Thereafter, on every public occasion – demonstration, assembly, or gala – Silvio Luparello had always shown up alongside the party bigwigs, but always one step behind them, half smiling as if to say that he stood there by choice, not out of hierarchical protocol. Officially drafted numerous times as a candidate in both the local and parliamentary elections, he had withdrawn every time for the noblest of reasons (always duly brought to the public's attention), invoking that humility, that desire to serve in silence and shadow, proper to every true Catholic. And in silence and shadow he had served for nearly twenty years, until the day when, fortified by all that his eagle eyes had seen in the shadow, he took a few servants of his own, first and foremost Deputy Cusumano. Later he would likewise get Senator Portolano and Chamber Deputy Tricomi to wear his livery (though the papers called them 'fraternal friends' and 'devoted followers'). In short, the whole party, in Montelusa and its province, had passed into his hands, as had some 80 per cent of all public and private contracts. Not even the earthquake unleashed by a handful of Milanese judges, unseating a political class that had been in power for fifty years, had touched him. On the contrary: having always remained in the background, he could now come out into the open, step into the light, and thunder against the corruption of his party cronies. In barely a year's time, as the standard-bearer for renewal, he had become provincial secretary, to the acclaim of the rank and file. Unfortunately, however, this glorious appointment had come a mere three days before his death. One newspaper lamented the fact that cruel fate had not granted a man of such lofty and exemplary stature the time needed to restore his party to its former splendour. In commemorating him, both newspapers together recalled his great generosity and kind-heartedness, his readiness to lend a hand, in any circumstance, to friend and foe alike, without partisan distinction.

With a shudder, Montalbano remembered a news story he'd seen the previous year on some local TV station. In the town of Belfi, his grandfather's birthplace, Luparello was dedicating a small orphanage, named after this same grandfather. Some twenty small children, all dressed alike, were singing a song of thanks to the engineer, who listened with visible emotion. The words of that little song had etched themselves indelibly in the inspector's memory:

What a good man,
What a fine fellow
Is our dear
Signor Luparello.

In addition to glossing over the circumstances of the engineer's death, the newspapers also carefully ignored the rumours that had been swirling for untold years around far less public affairs in which he'd been involved. There was talk of rigged contract competitions, kickbacks in the billions of lire, pressures applied to the point of extortion. And in all these instances the name that constantly popped up was that of Counsellor Rizzo, first the caddy, then the right-hand man, and finally the alter ego of Luparello. But these always remained rumours, voices in the air and on the wind. Some even said that Rizzo was a liaison between Luparello and the Mafia, and on this very subject the inspector had once managed to read a confidential report that spoke of currency smuggling and money laundering. Suspicions, of course, and nothing more, since they were never given a chance to be substantiated; every authorization request for an investigation had been lost in the labyrinths of that same courthouse the engineer's father had designed and built.

*

At lunchtime Montalbano phoned the Montelusa flying squad and asked to speak to Corporal Ferrara. She was the daughter of an old schoolmate of his who had married young, an attractive, sharp-witted girl who every now and then, for whatever reason, would try to seduce him.

'Anna? I need you.'

'What? I don't believe it.'

'Do you have a couple of free hours this afternoon?'

'I'll get them, Inspector. Always at your service, night and day. At your beck and call, even, or if you like, at your whim.'

'Good. I'll come and pick you up in Montelusa, at your house, around three.'

'This must be happiness.'

'Oh, and, Anna, wear feminine clothes.'

'Spike heels and slit dress, that sort of thing?'

'I just meant not in uniform.'

*

Punctually, at the second honk, Anna came out the front door in skirt and blouse. She didn't ask any questions and limited herself to kissing Montalbano on the cheek. Only when the car turned onto one of the three small byways that led from the provincial road to the Pasture did she speak.

'Um, if you want to fuck, let's go to your house. I don't like it here.'

At the Pasture there were only two or three cars, but the people inside them clearly did not belong to Gegè Gullotta's evening shift. They were students, boys and girls, married lovers who had nowhere else to go. Montalbano took the little road to the end, not stopping until the front tyres were already sinking into the sand. The large shrub next to which Luparello's BMW had been found was on their left but could not be reached by that route.

'Is that where they found him?' asked Anna.

'Yes.'

'What are you looking for?'

'I'm not sure. Let's get out.'

As they headed toward the water's edge, Montalbano put his arm around her waist and pressed her toward him; she rested her head on his shoulder, smiling. She now understood why the inspector had invited her along: it was all an act. Together they would look like a pair of lovers who had found a place to be alone at the Pasture. In their anonymity they would arouse no curiosity.

What a son of a bitch! she thought. *He doesn't give a shit about my feelings for him.*

At a certain point Montalbano stopped, his back to the sea. The shrub was in front of them, about a hundred yards away as the crow flies. There could be no doubt: the BMW had come not by way of the small roads but from the beach side and had stopped after circling toward the bush, its nose facing the old factory; that is, in the exact opposite position to that which all the other cars coming off the provincial road had to take, there being absolutely no room in which to manoeuvre. Anyone who wanted to return to the provincial road had no choice but to go back up the byway in reverse. Montalbano walked another short distance, his arm still around Anna, his head down: he could find no tyre tracks; the sea had erased everything.

'So what now?'

'First I have to call Fazio. Then I'll take you back home.'

'Inspector, may I tell you something in all honesty?'

'Of course.'

'You're an arsehole.'

FOUR

'Inspector? Pasquano here. Where the hell have you been hiding? I've been looking for you for three hours, and at headquarters they couldn't tell me anything.'

'Are you angry at me, Doctor?'

'At you? At the whole stinking universe!'

'What have they done to you?'

'They forced me to give priority to Luparello, the same way, exactly, as when he was alive. So even in death the guy has to come before everyone else? I suppose he's first in line at the cemetery, too?'

'Was there something you wanted to tell me?'

'Just an advance notice of what I'm going to send you in writing. Absolutely nothing: the dear departed died of natural causes.'

'Such as?'

'To put it in unscientific terms, his heart burst,

literally. In every other respect he was healthy, you know. It was only his pump that didn't work, and that's what screwed him, even though they made a valiant attempt to repair it.'

'Any other marks on the body?'

'What sort of marks?'

'I don't know, bruises, injections . . .'

'As I said, nothing. I wasn't born yesterday, you know. And anyway, I asked and obtained permission for my colleague Capuano, his regular doctor, to take part in the autopsy.'

'Covering your arse, eh Doc?'

'What did you say?'

'Something stupid, I'm sorry. Did he have any other ailments?'

'Why are you starting over from the top? There was nothing wrong with him, just a little high blood pressure. He treated it with a diuretic, took a pill every Thursday and Sunday, first thing in the morning.'

'So on Sunday, when he died, he had taken it?'

'So what? What the hell's that supposed to mean? That his diuretic pill had been poisoned? You think we're still living in the days of the Borgias? Or have you started reading remaindered mystery novels? If he'd been poisoned, don't you think I would have noticed?'

'Had he dined that evening?'

'No, he hadn't.'

'Can you tell me at what time he died?'

'You're going to drive me crazy with questions like that. You must be watching too many American movies, you know, where as soon as the cop asks what time the crime took place, the coroner tells him the murderer finished his work at six-thirty-two p.m., give or take a few seconds, thirty-six days ago. You saw with your own eyes that rigor mortis hadn't set in yet, didn't you? You felt how hot it was in that car, didn't you?'

'So?'

'So it's safe to say the deceased left this world between seven and nine o'clock the evening before he was found.'

'Nothing else?'

'Nothing else. Oh yes, I almost forgot: Mr Luparello died, of course, but he did manage to do it first – to have sex, that is. Traces of semen were found around his lower body.'

*

'Mr Commissioner? This is Montalbano. I wanted to let you know I just spoke with Dr Pasquano on the phone. The autopsy's been done.'

'Save your breath, Montalbano. I know everything already: around two o'clock I got a call from Jacomuzzi, who was there and filled me in. Wonderful, eh?'

'I'm sorry, I don't understand.'

'It's wonderful, that is, that someone in this fine province of ours should decide to die a natural death and thereby set a good example. Don't you think? Another two or three deaths like Luparello's and we'll start catching up with the rest of Italy. Have you spoken to Lo Bianco?'

'Not yet.'

'Please do so at once. Tell him there are no more problems as far as we're concerned. They can get on with the funeral whenever they like, if the judge gives the go-ahead. Listen, Montalbano – I forgot to mention it this morning – my wife has invented a fantastic new recipe for baby octopus. Can you make it Friday evening?'

*

'Montalbano? This is Lo Bianco. I wanted to bring you up to date on things. Early this afternoon I got a phone call from Dr Jacomuzzi.'

What a wasted career! Montalbano thought furiously to himself. *In another age he would have made an excellent town crier.*

'He told me the autopsy revealed nothing abnormal,' the judge continued. 'So I authorized burial. Do you have any objection?'

'None.'

'Can I therefore consider the case closed?'

'Think I could have two more days?'

He could hear the alarms ringing in the judge's head.

'Why, Montalbano? Is there something wrong?'

'No, Your Honour, nothing at all.'

'Well, why then, for the love of God? I'll confess to you, Inspector – I've no problem doing so – that I, as well as the chief prosecutor, the prefect, and the commissioner, have been strongly pressured to bring this affair to an end as quickly as possible. Nothing illegal, mind you. Urgent entreaties, all very proper, on the part of those – family, political friends – who want to forget the whole sad story as soon as possible. And they're right, in my opinion.'

'I understand, Your Honour. But I still need two days, no more.'

'But why? Give me a reason!'

He found an answer, a pretext. He couldn't very well tell the judge his request was founded on nothing, or rather on the feeling that he'd been hoodwinked – he didn't know how or why – by someone who at that moment was proving himself to be shrewder than he.

'If you really must know, it's out of concern for public opinion. I wouldn't want anyone to start whispering that we closed the case in haste because we had no intention of getting to the bottom of things. As you know, it doesn't take much to start people thinking that way.'

'If that's how you feel, then all right. You can have your forty-eight hours. But not a minute more. Try to understand the situation.'

*

'Gegè? How's it going, handsome? Sorry to wake you at six-thirty in the evening.'

'Fucking shit!'

'Gegè, is that any way to speak to a representative of the law? Especially someone like you, who before the law can only shit your pants? And speaking of fucking, is it true you're doing it with a ten-and-change black man?'

'Ten-and-change what?'

'Inches of cock.'

'Cut the shit. What do you want?'

'To talk to you.'

'When?'

'Tonight, late. You tell me what time.'

'Let's make it midnight.'

'Where?'

'The usual place, at Puntasecca.'

'A big kiss for your pretty lips, Gegè.'

*

'Inspector Montalbano? This is Prefect Squatrito. Judge Lo Bianco communicated to me just now that you asked for another twenty-four hours – or forty-eight, I can't remember – to close the case of the late Mr Luparello. Dr Jacomuzzi, who has politely kept me informed of all developments, told me that the autopsy established unequivocally that Luparello died of natural causes. Far be it from me to think – what am I saying, to even dream – of interfering in any way, since in any case there'd be no reason to do so, but do let me ask you: why this request?'

'My request, sir, as I have already explained to Justice Lo Bianco and will now reiterate, was dictated by a desire for transparency, to nip in the bud any malicious supposition that the police department might prefer not to clarify every aspect of the case and wish to close it without due verification of all leads. That's all.'

The prefect declared himself satisfied with the reply, and indeed Montalbano had carefully chosen two verbs ('clarify' and 'reiterate') and one noun ('transparency') which had forever been key words in the prefect's vocabulary.

*

'Hello? This is Anna, sorry to disturb you.'

'Why are you talking like that? Do you have a cold?'

'No, I'm at the squad office, but I don't want anyone to hear.'

'What is it?'

'Jacomuzzi called my boss and told him you don't want to close the Luparello case yet. The boss said you're just being an arsehole as usual, which I agree with and actually had a chance to tell you just a few hours ago.'

'Is that why you called? Thanks for the confirmation.'

'There's something else I have to tell you, Inspector, something I found out right after I left you, when I got back here.'

'Look, Anna, I'm up to my neck in shit. Tell me about it tomorrow.'

'There's no time to lose. It may be of interest to you.'

'I'm going to be busy here till one or one-thirty this morning. If you want to drop by now, then all right.'

'I can't make it right now. I'll see you at your place at two.'

'Tonight?!'

'Yes, and if you're not there, I'll wait.'

*

'Hello, darling? It's Livia. Sorry to call you at work, but—'

'You can call me whenever and wherever you want. What is it?'

'Nothing important. I was reading in a newspaper just now about the death of a politician in your parts. It's just a brief notice. It says that Inspector Salvo Montalbano is conducting a thorough investigation of the possible causes of death.'

'So?'

'Is this death causing you any problems?'

'Not too many.'

'So nothing's changed? You're still coming to see me on Saturday? You don't have some unpleasant surprise in store for me?'

'Like what?'

'Like an awkward phone call telling me the investigation has taken a new turn and so I'll have to wait but you don't know how long and so it's probably better to postpone everything for a week? It certainly wouldn't be the first time.'

'Don't worry, this time I'll manage.'

*

'Inspector Montalbano? This is Father Arcangelo Baldovino, secretary to His Excellency the bishop.'

'It's a pleasure. What can I do for you, Father?'

'The bishop has learned, with some astonishment, I must say, that you think it advisable to prolong your investigation into the sad and unfortunate passing of Silvio Luparello. Is this true?'

It was indeed, Montalbano confirmed, and for the third time he explained his reasons for acting in this manner. Father Baldovino seemed persuaded, yet begged the inspector to hurry up, 'to avoid untoward speculation and spare the already afflicted family yet another torment'.

*

'Inspector Montalbano? This is Mr Luparello.'

'What the hell! Didn't you die?' Montalbano was about to say, but he stopped himself in the nick of time.

'I'm his son,' the other continued, in a very educated, polite tone that had no trace of dialect whatsoever. 'My name is Stefano. I'm afraid I must appeal to your kindness and make what may seem to you an unusual request. I'm calling you on my mother's behalf.'

'By all means, if I can be of any help.'

'Mama would like to meet you.'

'What's unusual about that? I myself was intending to ask your mother if I could drop by sometime.'

'The thing is, Inspector, Mama would like to meet you by tomorrow at the latest.'

'My God, Mr Luparello, I really haven't got a single free moment these days, as you can imagine. And neither do you, I should think.'

'Don't worry, we can find ten minutes. How about tomorrow afternoon at five o'clock sharp?'

*

'Montalbano, sorry to make you wait, but I was—'

'On the toilet, in your element.'

'Come on, what do you want?'

'I wanted to let you in on something very serious. The pope just phoned me from the Vatican, really pissed off at you.'

'What are you talking about?!'

'He's furious because he's the only person in the world who hasn't received your report on the Luparello autopsy. He felt neglected and told me he intends to excommunicate you. You're screwed.'

'Montalbano, you've completely lost your mind.'

'Can you tell me something, just out of curiosity?'

'Sure.'

'Do you kiss arse out of ambition or natural inclination?'

'Natural inclination, I think.'

The sincerity of the response caught the inspector by surprise.

'Listen, have you finished examining the clothes Luparello was wearing? Did you find anything?'

'We found what you'd expect. Traces of semen on the underwear and trousers.'

'And inside the car?'

'We're still examining it.'

'Thanks. Now go back to the toilet.'

*

'Inspector? I'm calling from a phone booth on the provincial road, near the old factory. I did what you asked me to do.'

'Tell me about it, Fazio.'

'You were absolutely right. Luparello's BMW came from Montelusa, not Vigàta.'

'Are you certain?'

'On the Vigàta side, the beach is cordoned off by cement blocks. You can't get through. He would have had to fly.'

'Did you find out which way he might have come?'

'Yes, but it's totally crazy.'

'Why? Explain.'

'Because, even though from Montelusa to Vigàta there are dozens of roads and byways that one can take to avoid being seen, at a certain point, to get to the Pasture, Luparello's car would have had to pass through the dry bed of the Canneto.'

'The Canneto? But it's impassable!'

'Well, I did it, and therefore somebody else could have done it. It's completely dry. The only problem is, my car's suspension is ruined. And since you didn't want me to take a squad car, I'm going to have to—'

'I'll pay for the repairs myself. Anything else?'

'Yes. As it was pulling out of the riverbed and turning onto the sand, the BMW's tyres left some tracks. If we tell Jacomuzzi right away, we can get a cast of them.'

'Fuck Jacomuzzi. '

'Yes, sir. Need anything else?'

'No, Fazio, just come back to headquarters. And thanks.'

FIVE

The little beach of Puntasecca, a compact strip of sand sheltered by a hill of white marl, was deserted at that hour. When the inspector arrived, Gegè was already there waiting for him, leaning against his car and smoking a cigarette.

'Come on out, Salvù,' he said to Montalbano. 'Let's enjoy the fine night air a minute.'

They stood there a bit in silence, smoking. Then Gegè, having put out his cigarette, began to speak.

'I know what you want to ask me, Salvù. I'm well prepared. You can ask me anything you like, even jumping around.'

They smiled at this shared memory. They'd known each other since La Primina, the little private kindergarten where the teacher was Signorina Marianna, Gegè's sister, some fifteen years his senior. Salvo and

Gegè were listless schoolboys, learning their lessons like parrots, and like parrots repeating them in class. Some days, however, Signorina Marianna wasn't satisfied with those litanies, so she'd start jumping around in her questions; that is, she wouldn't follow the order in which the information had been presented. And this meant trouble, because then you had to have understood the material and grasped the logical connections.

'How's your sister doing?' asked Montalbano.

'I took her to Barcelona. There's a specialized eye clinic there. They say they can work miracles. They told me they can get the right eye, at least, to recover in part.'

'When you see her, give her my best.'

'I will. But as I was saying, I'm well prepared, so you can start firing away with the questions.'

'How many people do you have working for you at the Pasture?'

'Between whores and fags of various sorts, twenty-eight. Then there's Filippo di Cosmo and Manuele Lo Pìparo, who are there just to make sure there's no trouble. The smallest thing, you know, and I'm screwed.'

'You've got to keep your eyes open.'

'Right. Do you realize the kind of problems I'd have if there was a brawl or somebody got knifed or OD'd?'

'Still sticking to light drugs?'

'Yeah. Grass, coke at the most. Ask the street cleaners if they ever find a single syringe, go ahead and ask 'em.'

'I believe you.'

'Then there's Giambalvo, chief of vice, who's always breathing down my neck. He says he'll put up with me as long as I don't create any complications and bust his balls with something big.'

'I know Giambalvo. He doesn't want to have to shut down the Pasture or he'd lose his cut. What do you give him, a monthly wage? A fixed percentage? How much does he get?'

Gegè smiled.

'Get yourself transferred to vice and you'll find out. I'd like that. It'd give me a chance to help out a poor wretch like you, who lives only on his salary and goes around dressed in rags.'

'Thanks for the compliment. Now tell me about that night.'

'Well, it must have been around ten, ten-thirty, when Milly, who was working that night, saw some headlights coming from the Montelusa side near the sea, heading up toward the Pasture at a good clip. Freaked her out.'

'Who's this Milly?'

'Her real name's Giuseppina La Volpe, thirty years old, born at Mistretta. She's a smart girl.'

He took a folded-up sheet of paper out of his pocket and handed it to Montalbano.

'Here, I've written out everyone's real name. And address, too, in case you wanted to talk to somebody in person.'

'Why did you say Milly got scared?'

'Because there's no way a car could come from that direction, unless it passed through the Canneto, which would be a sure way to bust up your car and your arse into the bargain. At first she thought it was some brilliant idea of Giambalvo's, a surprise round-up or something. Then she realized it couldn't be vice: you don't do a round-up with only one squad car. So she got even more scared, because it occurred to her it might be the Monterosso boys, who've been waging war on me, trying to take the Pasture away, and maybe there would even be a shoot-out. So, to be ready to hightail it out of there at any moment, she kept her eyes on that car, and her client started complaining. But she had enough time to see that the car was turning and heading straight for the bushes nearby, driving almost into them. And then it stopped.'

'You're not telling me anything new, Gegè.'

'The guy who'd been fucking Milly then dropped her off and went back up the path, in reverse, to the provincial road. Milly waited around for another trick, walking back and forth. Then Carmen arrived at the spot where she'd been a minute before, with a devoted client who comes to see her at the same time every Saturday and Sunday and spends hours with her. Carmen's real name is on that piece of paper I gave you.'

'Her address, too?'

'Yes. Before the client turned off his headlights, Carmen noticed that the two inside the BMW were already fucking.'

'Did she tell you exactly what she saw?'

'Yes. It was only a few seconds, but she got a good look. Maybe because it had made an impression on her, since you don't usually see cars like that at the

Pasture. Anyway, the girl, who was in the driver's seat – oh, I forgot to mention, Milly said it was the girl who was driving – she turned, climbed onto the lap of the man beside her, fiddling around with her hands underneath, but you couldn't see them, and then she started going up and down. You haven't forgotten how people fuck, have you?'

'I don't think so, but we can check. When you've finished telling me what you've got to tell me, drop your pants, put your pretty little hands on the trunk, and stick your arse up in the air. If I've forgotten anything, you can remind me. Now go on, and stop wasting my time.'

'When they were done, the girl opened the car door and got out, straightened her skirt, and shut the door. The man, instead of starting up the car and leaving, stayed where he was, with his head leaning back. The girl passed very close by Carmen's car, and at that exact moment a car's headlights shone right on her. She was a good-looking lady, blonde, well dressed, and she had a shoulder bag in her left hand. Then she headed toward the old factory.'

'Anything else?'

'Yes. Manuele, who was making the rounds in his

car, saw her leave the Pasture and walk toward the provincial road. Since she didn't look to him like Pasture material, by the way she was dressed, he turned around to follow her, but then a car came by and picked her up.'

'Wait a second, Gegè. Did Manuele see her standing there, with her thumb out, waiting for someone to give her a ride?'

'Salvù, how do you do it? You really are a born cop.'

'Why do you say that?'

'Because that's exactly the point Manuele's not convinced about. In other words, he didn't see the chick make any signal, but the car did stop. And that's not all: although the car was moving along at a pretty good clip, Manuele had the impression the door was already open when it put on the brakes to pick her up. But Manuele didn't think to take down the licence number – there wasn't any reason.'

'Right. And what can you tell me about the man in the BMW, Luparello?'

'Not much. He wore glasses, and he never took his jacket off to fuck, even though it was hot as hell. But there's one point where Milly's story and Carmen's don't jibe. Milly says that when the car arrived, it looked like the man had a tie or a black cravat around his neck; Carmen maintains that when she saw him, he had his shirt unbuttoned and that was all. But that seems like an unimportant detail to me, since Luparello could have taken off the tie while he was fucking. Maybe it bothered him.'

'His tie but not his jacket? But that's not unimportant, Gegè, because no tie or cravat was found inside the car.'

'That doesn't mean anything. Maybe it fell out onto the sand when the girl got out.'

'Jacomuzzi's men combed the area and didn't find anything.'

They stood there in silence, thoughtful.

'Maybe there's another explanation for what Milly saw,' Gegè suddenly said. 'Maybe it was never a question of ties or cravats. Maybe the man still had his seat belt on – after all, they'd just driven along the bed of the Canneto, with all its rocks and sticks – and he took it off when the girl climbed onto his lap, since the seat belt would surely have been a bother.'

'It's possible.'

'I've told you everything I was able to find out

about this, Salvù. And I tell you in my own interest. Because for a big cheese like Luparello to come and croak at the Pasture isn't good for business. Now everybody's eyes are gonna be on it, so the sooner you finish your investigation, the better. After a couple of days people forget, and we can all go back to work in peace. Can I go now? These are peak hours at the Pasture.'

'Wait. What's your opinion of the whole thing?'

'Me? You're the cop. But just to make you happy, I will say that the whole thing stinks to me. Let's imagine the girl is a high-class whore, a foreigner. Are you gonna tell me Luparello doesn't have a place to take her?'

'Gegè, do you know what a perversion is?'

'You're asking me? I could tell you a few things that would make you puke on my shoes. I know what you're going to say, that they came to the Pasture because they thought it would make it more erotic. And that does happen sometimes. Did you know that one night a judge showed up with his bodyguards?'

'Really? Who was it?'

'Judge Cosentino. See, I can even tell you the name. The evening before he was kicked out of office, he came to the Pasture with an escort car, picked up a transvestite, and had sex with him.'

'What did the bodyguards do?'

'They went for a long walk on the beach. But to get back to the subject: Cosentino knew he was a marked man and decided to have a little fun. But what interest could Luparello have had? He wasn't that kind of guy. Everybody knows he liked the ladies, but he was always careful never to let anyone see him. And where is the woman who could make him risk everything he had and everything he stood for just to get laid? I don't buy it, Salvù.'

'Go on.'

'If we suppose, on the other hand, that the chick was not a whore, then I really don't know. It's even less likely – downright impossible – they'd let themselves be seen at the Pasture. Also, the car was driven by the girl, that much is certain. Aside from the fact that no one would ever trust a whore with a car like that, that lady must have been something to strike fear in a man's heart. First of all, she has no problem driving down into the Canneto, and then, when Luparello dies between her thighs, she gets up like nothing, closes the door, and walks away. Does that seem normal to you?'

'I don't think so.'

At this point Gegè started laughing and flicked on his cigarette lighter.

'What are you doing?' asked Montalbano.

'Come over here, faggot. Bring your face to the light.'

The inspector obeyed, and Gegè illuminated his eyes. Then he extinguished the lighter.

'I get it. All along, you, a man of the law, were thinking the exact same thoughts as me, a man of crime. And you just wanted to see if they matched up. Eh, Salvù?'

'You guessed right.'

'I'm hardly ever wrong when it comes to you. Gotta go now. Ciao.'

'Thanks,' said Montalbano.

The inspector left first, but a moment later his friend pulled up beside him, gesturing for him to slow down.

'What do you want?'

'I don't know where my head was. I wanted to tell you this before. Do you have any idea what a pretty sight you made this afternoon, hand in hand with Corporal Ferrara?'

Then he accelerated, putting a safe distance between himself and the inspector, his arm waving goodbye.

*

Back at home, Montalbano jotted down a few of the details that Gegè had provided, but tiredness soon came over him. He glanced at his watch, noticed it was a little past one, and went to bed. The insistent ringing of the doorbell woke him up. His eyes looked over at the alarm clock: two-fifteen. He got up with some effort; the early stages of sleep always slowed down his reflexes.

'Who the fuck is that, at this hour?'

He went to the door just as he was, in his underpants, and opened up.

'Hi,' said Anna.

He'd completely forgotten; the girl had indeed said that she would come see him around this hour. Anna was looking him over.

'I see you're wearing the right clothes,' she said, then stepped inside.

'Say what it is you have to tell me, then go back home. I'm dead tired.'

Montalbano was truly annoyed by the intrusion. He went into his bedroom, put on a pair of trousers and a shirt, and returned to the dining room. Anna wasn't there. She had gone into the kitchen, opened the refrigerator, and was already sinking her teeth into a bread roll filled with prosciutto.

'I'm so hungry I can hardly see.'

'You can talk while you're eating.'

Montalbano put the espresso pot on the stove.

'You're going to make coffee? At this hour? Will you be able to fall back asleep afterwards?'

'Anna, please.' He was unable to be polite.

'All right. This afternoon, after we split up, I found out from a colleague, who for his part had been told by an informer, that starting yesterday, Tuesday morning, some guy's been going around to all the jewellers, receivers of stolen goods, and pawnbrokers both legitimate and illegitimate to alert them that if someone came in to buy or pawn a certain piece of jewellery, they should let him know. The piece in question is a necklace, with a solid-gold chain and a heart-shaped pendant covered with diamonds. The kind of thing you'd find at some cheap department store, except that this one's real.'

'So how are they supposed to let him know? By phone?'

'It's no joke. He told each one of them to give a different signal – I don't know, like putting a green cloth in the window or hanging a piece of newspaper from the front door, things like that. He's shrewd: that way he can see without being seen.'

'Fine, but I think—'

'Let me finish. From the way he spoke and acted, the people he approached concluded it was best to do as he said. Then we found out that some other people, at the same time, were making the same rounds in all the towns of the province, Vigàta included. Therefore, whoever lost that necklace wants it back.'

'Nothing wrong with that. So why, in your opinion, should this interest me?'

'Because the man told a certain receiver in Montelusa that the necklace might have been lost in the Pasture on Sunday night or Monday morning. Does it interest you now?'

'Up to a point.'

'I know, it may be only a coincidence and have nothing whatsoever to do with Luparello's death.'

'Thanks anyway. Now go back home. It's late.'

The coffee was ready. Montalbano poured himself a cup, and Anna naturally took advantage of the opportunity.

'None for me?'

With the patience of a saint, the inspector filled another cup and handed it to her. He liked Anna, but couldn't she understand he was with another woman?

'No,' Anna said suddenly, putting down her coffee.

'No what?'

'I don't want to go home. Would you really mind so much if I stayed here with you?'

'Yes, I would.'

'But why?'

'Because I'm too good a friend of your father. I'd feel like I was doing him wrong.'

'What bullshit!'

'It may be bullshit, but that's the way it is. And anyway, you seem to be forgetting that I'm in love, really in love, with another woman.'

'Who's not here.'

'She's not here, but it's as if she were. Now don't

be silly and don't say silly things. You're unlucky, Anna; you're up against an honest man. I'm sorry. Forgive me.'

*

He couldn't fall asleep. Anna had been right to warn him that the coffee would keep him awake. But something else was getting on his nerves: if that necklace had indeed been lost at the Pasture, then surely Gegè must also have been told about it. But Gegè had been careful not to mention it, and surely not because it was a meaningless detail.

SIX

At five-thirty in the morning, after having spent the night repeatedly getting up and going back to bed, Montalbano decided on a plan for Gegè, one that would indirectly pay him back for his silence about the lost necklace and his joke about the visit he'd made that afternoon to the Pasture. He took a long shower, drank three coffees in succession, then got in his car. When he arrived in Rabàto, the oldest quarter of Montelusa, destroyed thirty years earlier by a landslide and now consisting mostly of ruins refurbished and damaged higgledy-piggledy ramshackle hovels inhabited by illegal aliens from Tunisia and Morocco, he headed through narrow, tortuous alleyways toward Piazza Santa Croce. The church stood whole amid the ruins. He took from his pocket the sheet of paper Gegè had given him: Carmen, known in the real world as Fatma Ben Gallud, Tunisian, lived at number 48. It was a miserable *catojo,* a small ground-floor room with a little window in the wooden door to allow the air to circulate. He knocked: no answer. He knocked harder, and this time a sleepy voice asked, 'Who that?'

'Police,' Montalbano fired back. He had decided to play rough, catching her still drowsy from the sudden awakening. Certainly Fatma, because of her work at the Pasture, must have slept even less than he. The door opened, the woman covering herself in a large beach towel that she held up at breast level with one hand.

'What you want?'

'To talk to you.'

She stood aside. In the *catojo* there was a double bed half unmade, a little table with two chairs and a small gas stove. A plastic curtain separated the toilet and sink from the rest of the room. Everything was so clean and orderly it sparkled. But the smell of the woman and her cheap perfume so filled the room that one could hardly breathe.

'Let me see your residence permit.'

As if in fear, the woman let the towel fall as she brought her hands to her face to cover her eyes. Long legs, slim waist, flat belly, high, firm breasts – a real woman, in short, the type you see in television commercials. After a moment or two, Montalbano realized, from Fatma's expectant immobility, that what he was witnessing was not fear, but an attempt to reach the most obvious and common of arrangements between man and woman.

'Get dressed.'

There was a metal wire hung from one corner of the room to another. Fatma walked over to it: broad shoulders, perfect back, small, round buttocks.

With a body like that, thought Montalbano, *I bet she's been through it all.*

He imagined the men lining up discreetly in certain offices, with Fatma earning 'the indulgence of the authorities' behind closed doors, as he had happened several times to read about, an indulgence of the most self-indulgent kind. Fatma put on a light cotton dress over her naked body and remained standing in front of Montalbano.

'So . . . your papers?'

The woman shook her head no, and began to weep in silence.

'Don't be afraid,' the inspector said.

'I not afraid. I very unlucky.'

'Why?'

'Because you wait few days, I no here no more.'

'And where did you want to go?'

'Man from Fela he like me, I like him, he say Sunday he marry me. I believe him.'

'The man who comes to see you every Saturday and Sunday?'

Fatma's eyes widened.

'How you know?'

She started crying again.

'But now everything finish.'

'Tell me something. Is Gegè going to let you go with this man from Fela?'

'Man talk to Signor Gegè, man pay.'

'Listen, Fatma, pretend I never came to see you here. I only want to ask you one thing, and if you answer me truthfully, I will turn around and walk out of here, and you can go back to sleep.'

'What you want to know?'

'Did they ask you, at the Pasture, if you'd found anything?'

The woman's eyes lit up.

'Oh, yes! Signor Filippo come – he Signor Gegè's

man – tell us if we find gold necklace with heart of diamond, we give it straight to him. If not find, then look.'

'And do you know if it was found?'

'No. Also tonight, all girls look.'

'Thank you,' said Montalbano, heading for the door. In the doorway he stopped and turned round to look at Fatma.

'Good luck.'

So Gegè had been foiled. What he had so carefully neglected to mention to Montalbano, the inspector had managed to find out anyway. And from what Fatma had just told him, he drew a logical conclusion.

*

When he arrived at headquarters at the crack of dawn, the officer on guard gave him a look of concern.

'Anything wrong, Chief?'

'Nothing at all,' he reassured him. 'I just woke up early.'

He had bought the two Sicilian newspapers and sat down to read them. With a great wealth of detail, the first announced that the funeral service for Luparello would be held the following day. The solemn ceremony would take place at the cathedral, officiated by the bishop himself. Special security measures would be taken, due to the anticipated arrival of numerous important personages come to express their condolences and pay their last respects. At the latest count they would include two government ministers, four under-secretaries, eighteen members of parliament between senators and deputies, and a throng of regional deputies. And so city police, carabinieri, coastguard agents and traffic cops would all be called into action, to say nothing of personal bodyguards and other even more personal escorts, of which the newspaper mentioned nothing, made up of people who certainly had some connection with law and order, but from the other side of the barricade on top of which stood the law. The second newspaper more or less repeated the same things, while adding that the casket had been set up in the atrium of the Luparello mansion and that an endless line of people were waiting to express their thanks for everything the deceased had dutifully and impartially done – when still alive, of course.

Meanwhile Sergeant Fazio had arrived, and Montalbano spoke to him at great length about a number of investigations currently under way. No phone calls came in from Montelusa. Soon it was noon, and the inspector opened a file containing the deposition of the two garbage collectors concerning their discovery of the corpse. He copied down their addresses, said goodbye to the sergeant and the other policemen, and told them they'd hear from him in the afternoon.

If Gegè's men had talked to the whores about the necklace, they must certainly have said something to the garbage collectors as well.

*

Number 28 Gravet Terrace was a three-storey building, with an intercom at the front door. A mature woman's voice answered.

'I'm a friend of Pino's.'

'My son's not here.'

'Didn't he get off work?'

'He got off, but he went somewhere else.'

'Could you let me in, signora? I only want to leave him an envelope. What floor is it?'

'Top floor.'

A dignified poverty: two rooms, eat-in kitchen, bathroom. One could calculate the square footage the minute one entered. Pino's mother, fiftyish and modestly attired, showed him in.

'Pino's room's this way.'

A small room full of books and magazines, a little table covered with paper by the window.

'Where did Pino go?'

'To Raccadali. He's auditioning for a part in a play by Martoglio, the one about St John getting his head cut off. Pino really likes the theatre, you know.'

Montalbano approached the little table. Apparently Pino was writing a play; on a sheet of paper he had lined up a column of dialogue. But when he read one of the names, the inspector felt a kind of shock run through him.

'Signora, could I please have a glass of water?'

As soon as the woman left, he folded up the page and put it in his pocket.

'The envelope?' Pino's mother reminded him when she returned, handing him his water.

Montalbano then executed a perfect pantomime, one that Pino, had he been present, would have admired: he searched first in the pockets of his trousers, then more hastily in his jacket, whereupon he gave a look of surprise and finally slapped his forehead noisily.

'What an idiot! I left the envelope at the office! Just give me five minutes, signora, I'll be right back.'

Slipping into his car, he took out the page he'd just stolen, and what he read there darkened his mood. He restarted the engine and left. 102 Via Lincoln. In his deposition Saro had even specified the apartment number. With a bit of simple maths, the inspector figured that the surveyor/garbage collector must live on the sixth floor. The front door to the block was open, but the elevator was broken. He had to climb up six flights of stairs but had the satisfaction of having guessed right: a polished little plaque there read BALDASSARE MONTAPERTO. A tiny young woman answered the door with a baby in her arms and a worried look in her eye.

'Is Saro home?'

'He went to the drugstore to buy some medicine for the baby, but he'll be right back.'

'Is he sick?'

Without answering, she held her arm out slightly to let him see. The little thing was sick, and how: sallow, hollow-cheeked, with big, already grown-up eyes staring angrily at him. Montalbano felt terrible. He couldn't stand to see children suffer.

'What's wrong with him?'

'The doctors can't explain it. Who are you, sir?'

'The name's Virduzzo. I'm the accountant at Splendour.'

'Come on in.'

The woman felt reassured. The apartment was a mess, it being all too clear that Saro's wife was too busy always attending to the little boy to look after the house.

'What do you want with Saro?'

'I believe I made a mistake, on the minus side, on the amount of his last payslip. I'd like to see the stub.'

'If that's all you need,' said the woman, 'there's no need to wait for Saro. I can get you the stub myself. Come.'

Montalbano followed her, ready with another excuse to stay until the husband returned. There was a nasty smell in the bedroom, as of rotten milk. The woman tried to open the top drawer of a commode but was unable to, having only one free hand to use, as she was holding the baby in her other arm.

'I can do it, if you like,' said Montalbano.

The woman stepped aside, and the inspector opened the drawer and saw that it was full of papers, bills, prescriptions, receipts.

'Where are the payment envelopes?'

At that moment Saro entered the bedroom. They hadn't heard him come in; the front door to the apartment had been left open. The instant he saw Montalbano rummaging in the drawer, he was convinced the inspector was searching their house for the necklace. He turned pale, started trembling, and leaned against the door frame.

'What do you want?' he barely managed to articulate.

Frightened by her husband's obvious terror, the woman spoke before Montalbano had a chance to answer.

'But it's Virduzzo, the accountant!' she almost yelled.

'Virduzzo? That's Inspector Montalbano!'

The woman tottered, and Montalbano rushed forward to support her, fearing the baby might end up on the floor together with his mother. He helped sit her down on the bed. Then he spoke, the words coming out of his mouth without the intervention of his brain, a phenomenon that had come over him before and which one imaginative journalist had once called 'that flash of intuition which now and then strikes our policeman'.

'Where'd you put the necklace?' he said.

Saro stepped forward, stiff from struggling to remain standing on his pudding-legs, went over to his bedside table, opened the drawer, and pulled out a packet wrapped in newspaper, which he threw on the bed. Montalbano picked it up, went into the kitchen, sat down, and unwrapped the packet. The jewel was at once vulgar and very fine: vulgar in its design and conception, fine in its workmanship and in the cut of the diamonds with which it was studded. Saro, meanwhile, had followed him into the kitchen.

'When did you find it?'

'Early Monday morning, at the Pasture.'

'Did you tell anyone?'

'No, sir, just my wife.'

'And has anyone come to ask if you found a necklace like this?'

'Yes, sir. Filippo di Cosmo came. He's one of Gegè Gullotta's men.'

'And what did you tell him?'

'I said I hadn't found anything.'

'Did he believe you?'

'Yes, sir, I think so. Then he said that if I happened to find it, I should give it to him right away and not mess around, because it was a very sensitive matter.'

'Did he promise you anything?'

'Yes, sir. A deadly beating if I found it and kept it, fifty thousand lire if I found it and turned it over to him.'

'What did you plan to do with the necklace?'

'I wanted to pawn it. That's what Tana and I decided.'

'You weren't planning to sell it?'

'No, sir, it didn't belong to us. We saw it like something somebody had lent to us; we didn't want to profit from it.'

'We're honest people,' said the wife, who'd just come in, wiping her eyes.

'What were you going to do with the money?'

'We wanted to use it to treat our son. We could have taken him far away from here, to Rome, Milan – anywhere there might be doctors who know something.'

They were all silent a few moments. Then Montalbano asked the woman for two sheets of paper, which she tore out of a notebook they used for shopping expenses. Holding out one of the sheets to Saro, the inspector said, 'Make me a drawing that shows the exact spot where you found the necklace. You're a land surveyor, aren't you?'

As Saro was sketching, on the other sheet Montalbano wrote:

> I the undersigned, Salvo Montalbano, Chief Inspector of the Police Department of Vigàta (province of Montelusa), hereby declare having received on this day, from Mr Baldassare 'Saro' Montaperto, a solid-gold necklace with a heart-shaped pendant, also solid gold but studded with diamonds, found by Mr Montaperto around the area known as 'the Pasture' during the course of his work as ecological agent. In witness whereof,

And he signed, but paused a moment to reflect before adding the date at the bottom. Then he made up his mind and wrote, 'Vigàta, September 9, 1993.' Meanwhile Saro had finished. They exchanged sheets.

'Perfect,' said the inspector, looking over the detailed drawing.

'Here, however, the date is wrong,' Saro said. 'The ninth was last Monday. Today is the eleventh.'

'No, nothing wrong there. You brought that necklace into my office the same day you found it. You had it in your pocket when you came to police headquarters to tell me you'd found Luparello dead, but you didn't give it to me till later because you didn't want your fellow worker to see. Is that clear?'

'If you say so, sir.'

'Take good care of this statement.'

'What are you going to do now? Arrest him?' asked the woman.

'Why? What's he done?' asked Montalbano, standing up.

SEVEN

Montalbano was well respected at the San Calogero trattoria, not so much because he was a police inspector as because he was a good customer with discerning tastes. Today they fed him some very fresh striped mullet, fried to a delicate crisp and drained on absorbent paper. After coffee and a long stroll on the eastern jetty, he went back to the office. Fazio got up from his desk as soon as he saw him.

'There's someone waiting for you, Chief.'

'Who is it?'

'Pino Catalane, remember him? One of the two garbage collectors who found Luparello's body.'

'Send him right in.'

He immediately noticed that the youth was tense, nervous.

'Have a seat.'

Pino sat with his buttocks on the edge of the chair.

'Could you tell me why you came to my house and put on the act that you did? I've got nothing to hide.'

'I did it simply to avoid frightening your mother. If I told her I was a police inspector, she might've had a heart attack.'

'Well, in that case, thanks.'

'How did you figure out it was me who was looking for you?'

'I phoned my mother to see how she was feeling – when I left her she had a headache – and she told me a man had come to give me an envelope but forgot to bring it with him. She said he'd gone out to get it but had never come back. I became curious and asked her to describe the guy. When you're trying to pretend you're somebody else, you should cover up that mole you've got under your left eye. What do you want from me?'

'I have a question. Did anyone come to the Pasture to ask if you'd found a necklace?'

'Yes, someone you know, in fact: Filippo di Cosmo.'

'What did you say?'

'I told him I hadn't found it, which was the truth.'

'And what did he say?'

'He said if I found it, so much the better for me, he'd give me fifty thousand lire, but if I found it and I didn't turn it over to him, so much the worse. He said the same thing to Saro. But Saro didn't find it either.'

'Did you go home before coming here?'

'No, sir, I came here directly.'

'Do you write for the theatre?'

'No, but I like to act now and then.'

'Then what's this?'

Montalbano handed him the page he'd taken from the little table. Pino looked at it, unimpressed, and smiled.

'No, that's not a theatre scene, that's . . . '

He fell silent, at a loss. It occurred to him that if those weren't lines of dramatic dialogue, he would have to explain what they were, and it wouldn't be easy.

'I'll help you out,' said Montalbano. 'This is a transcript of a phone call one of you made to Rizzo, the lawyer, right after you found Luparello's body, before you came here to headquarters to report your discovery. Am I right?'

'Yes, sir.'

'Who made the phone call?'

'I did. But Saro was right beside me, listening.'

'Why'd you do it?'

'Because Luparello was an important person, a big cheese. So we immediately thought we should inform Rizzo. Actually, no, the first person we thought of calling was Deputy Cusumano.'

'Why didn't you?'

'Because Cusumano, with Luparello dead, was like somebody who, when an earthquake hits, loses not only his house but also the money he was keeping under the floorboards.'

'Give me a better explanation of why you called Rizzo.'

'Because we thought maybe something could still be done.'

'Like what?'

Pino didn't answer, but only passed his tongue over his lips.

'I'll help you out again. You said maybe something could still be done. Something like moving the car out of the Pasture and letting the body be found somewhere else? Were you thinking that's what Rizzo might ask you to do?'

'Yes.'

'And you would have been willing to do it?'

'Of course! That's why we called!'

'What did you expect to get out of it?'

'We were hoping maybe he could find us other jobs, or help us win some competition for surveyors, or find us the right job, so we wouldn't have to work as stinking garbage collectors any more. You know as well as I do, Inspector, you can't sail without a favourable wind.'

'Now explain the most important thing: why did you write down that conversation? Were you hoping to blackmail him with it?'

'How? With words? Words are just air.'

'So what was your reason?'

'Well, believe it or not, I wrote down that conversation because I wanted to study it. Something didn't sound right to me – speaking as a man of the theatre, that is.'

'I don't follow.'

'Let's pretend that what's written down is supposed

to be staged. I'm the Pino character, and I phone the Rizzo character early in the morning to tell him I've just found his boss dead. He's the guy's secretary, his devoted friend, his political crony. He's more than a brother. But the Rizzo character, he keeps cool as a cucumber, doesn't get upset, doesn't ask where we found him, how he died, if he was shot, if he died in a car crash, nothing. He only asks why we've come to him, of all people, with the news. Does that sound right to you?'

'No. Go on.'

'He shows no surprise, in other words. In fact, he tries to put a distance between himself and the dead man, as if this was just some passing acquaintance of his. And he immediately tells us to do our duty, which is to call the police. Then he hangs up. No, Inspector, as drama it's all wrong. The audience would just laugh. It doesn't work.'

Montalbano dismissed Pino and kept the sheet of paper. When the garbage collector left, he reread it.

It did work, and how. It worked marvellously, if in this hypothetical drama – which in the end was not really so hypothetical – Rizzo, before receiving the phone call, already knew where and how Luparello had died and anxiously wanted the body to be discovered as quickly as possible.

*

Jacomuzzi gaped at Montalbano, astonished. The inspector stood before him, dressed to the nines: dark-blue suit, white shirt, burgundy tie, sparkling black shoes.

'Jesus! Going to your wedding?'

'Have you done with Luparello's car? What did you find?'

'Nothing of importance inside. But—'

'The suspension was broken.'

'How did you know?'

'A little bird told me. Listen, Jacomuzzi.'

He pulled the necklace out of his pocket and tossed it onto the table. Jacomuzzi picked it up, looked at it carefully, and made a gesture of surprise.

'But this is real! It's worth tens of millions of lire! Was it stolen?'

'No, somebody found it on the ground at the Pasture and brought it in to me.'

'At the Pasture? What kind of whore can afford a piece of jewellery like that? You must be kidding!'

'I want you to examine it, photograph it, do all the little things you usually do. Then bring me the results as soon as you can.'

The telephone rang. Jacomuzzi answered and passed the receiver to his colleague.

'Who is it?'

'It's Fazio, Chief. Come back to town immediately. All hell's breaking loose.'

'What is it?'

'Contino the schoolteacher's shooting at people.'

'What do you mean, shooting?'

'Shooting shooting! He fired two shots from the balcony of his apartment at the people sitting at the café below, screaming something nobody could understand. Then he fired another shot at me as I was coming through his front door to see what was going on.'

'Has he killed anyone?'

'No. He just grazed the arm of a certain De Francesco.'

'OK, I'll be right there.'

*

As he travelled the six miles back to Vigàta at breakneck speed, Montalbano thought of Contino the schoolteacher. Not only did he know him, there was a secret between them. Six months earlier the inspector had been taking the stroll he customarily allowed himself two or three times a week along the eastern jetty, out to the lighthouse. Before he set out, however, he always stopped at Anselmo Greco's shop, a hovel that clashed with the clothing boutiques and shiny, mirrored cafés along the *corso.* Among such antiquated items as terracotta dolls and rusty weights for nineteenth-century scales, Greco also sold *càlia e simenza,* a mixture of roasted chickpeas and salted pumpkin seeds. Montalbano would buy a paper cone full of these and then head out. That day, after he had reached the point, he was turning around, right under the lighthouse, when he saw an elderly man beneath him, sitting on a block of the low concrete breakwater, head down, immobile. Montalbano got a better look, to see if perhaps the man was holding a fishing line in his hands. But he wasn't fishing; he wasn't doing anything. Suddenly he stood up, quickly made the sign of the cross, and balanced himself on his tiptoes.

'Stop!' Montalbano shouted.

The man froze; he had thought he was alone. In

a couple of bounds Montalbano reached him, grabbed him by the lapels of his jacket, lifted him up bodily, and carried him to safety.

'What were you trying to do, kill yourself?'

'Yes.'

'Why?'

'Because my wife is cheating on me.'

This was the last thing Montalbano expected to hear. The man had surely passed his eightieth year.

'How old is your wife?'

'Let's say eighty. I'm eighty-two.'

An absurd conversation in an absurd situation, and the inspector didn't feel like continuing it. Taking the man by the arm, he forced him to walk toward town. At this point, just to make everything even crazier, the man introduced himself.

'I am Giosuè Contino, if I may. I used to teach elementary school. Who are you? If, of course, you wish to tell me.'

'My name is Salvo Montalbano. I'm police inspector for the town of Vigàta.'

'Oh, really? Then you came at just the right time. You yourself can tell my slut of a wife she'd better stop cuckolding me with Agatino De Francesco or one of these days I'm going to do something crazy.'

'And who's this De Francesco?'

'He used to be the postman. He's younger than I am, seventy-six years old, and he has a pension that's one and a half times the size of mine.'

'Do you know this to be a fact, or are you just suspicious?'

'I'm absolutely certain it's the gospel truth. Every afternoon God sends our way, rain or shine, this De Francesco comes and has a coffee at the café right under my house.'

'So what?'

'How long do *you* take to drink a cup of coffee?'

For a minute Montalbano went along with the old schoolmaster's quiet madness.

'That depends. If I'm standing—'

'What's that got to do with it? When you're sitting!'

'Well, it depends on whether I have an appointment and have to wait, or if I only want to pass the time.'

'No, my friend, that man sits there only to eye

my wife, who eyes him back, and they never waste an opportunity to do so.'

They had arrived back in town.

'Where do you live, Mr Contino?'

'At the end of the *corso,* on Piazza Dante.'

'Let's take a back street, I think that's better.' Montalbano didn't want the sodden, shivering old man to arouse the townspeople's curiosity and questions.

'Coming upstairs with me? Would you like a coffee?' he asked the inspector while extracting the front-door keys from his pocket.

'No, thanks. Just dry yourself off and change your clothes.'

That same evening he had gone to speak with De Francesco, the ex-postman, a tiny, unpleasant old man who reacted quite harshly to the inspector's advice, screaming in his face.

'I'll take my coffee wherever and whenever I like! What, is it illegal to go sit at the café under that arteriosclerotic Contino's balcony? You surprise me, sir. You're supposed to represent the law, and instead you come and tell me these things!'

*

'It's all over,' said the municipal policeman keeping curious bystanders away from the front door on Piazza Dante. At the entrance to the apartment stood Sergeant Fazio, who threw his arms up in distress. The rooms were in perfect order, sparkling clean. Master Contino was lying in an armchair, a small bloodstain over his heart. The revolver was on the floor, next to the armchair, an ancient Smith & Wesson five-shooter that must have dated back at least to the time of Buffalo Bill but which unfortunately still worked. His wife was lying on the bed, she, too, with a bloodstain over her heart, her hands clasped around a rosary. She must have been praying before agreeing to let her husband kill her. Montalbano thought again of the commissioner, who this time was right: here death had indeed found its dignity.

*

Nervous and surly, Montalbano gave the sergeant his instructions and left him there to wait for the judge. He felt, aside from a sudden melancholy, a subtle remorse: if only he had intervened more wisely with the schoolmaster, if only he had alerted Contino's friends and doctor in time . . .

*

He took a long walk along the wharf and the eastern jetty, his favourite. His spirits slightly revived, he returned to the office. There he found Fazio beside himself.

'What is it? What's happened? Hasn't the judge come yet?'

'No, he came, and they've already taken the bodies away.'

'So what's wrong?'

'What's wrong is that while half the town was watching Contino shoot his gun, some bastards went into action and cleaned out two apartments top to bottom. I've already sent four of our men. I was waiting for you to show up so I could go and join them.'

'All right, go. I'll be here.'

He decided it was time to play his ace: the trap he had in mind couldn't fail. He reached for the phone.

'Jacomuzzi?'

'What, for God's sake! What's the rush? I still don't have any report on your necklace. It's too early.'

'I'm well aware you couldn't possibly tell me anything yet, I realize that.'

'So what do you want?'

'To advise you to maintain total secrecy. The story behind that necklace is not as simple as it may appear. It could lead to unexpected developments.'

'You insult me! If you tell me not to talk about something, I won't talk about it, even if the heavens fall!'

*

'Mr Luparello? I'm so sorry I couldn't come today. It simply wasn't possible, you must believe me. Please extend my apologies to your mother.'

'Just a minute, Inspector.'

Montalbano waited patiently.

'Inspector? Mama says tomorrow at the same hour, if that's all right with you.'

It was all right with him, and he confirmed the appointment.

EIGHT

He returned home tired, intending to go straight to bed, but almost mechanically – it was sort of a tic – he turned on the television. The Televigàta anchorman, after talking about the event of the day, a shoot-out between petty Mafiosi on the outskirts of Miletta a few hours earlier, announced that the provincial secretariat of the party to which Luparello belonged (actually, used to belong) had convened in Montelusa. It was a highly unusual meeting, one that in less turbulent times than these would have been held, out of due respect for the deceased, at least thirty days after his passing; but things being what they were, the troubling situation called for quick, lucid decisions. And so a new provincial secretary had been elected, unanimously: Dr Angelo Cardamone, chief osteologist at Montelusa Hospital, a man who had always fought with Luparello from within the party, but fairly and courageously and always out in the open. This clash of ideas – the newsman continued – could be simplified in the following terms: Engineer Luparello was in favour of maintaining the four-party governing coalition while allowing the introduction of pristine new forces untrammelled by politics (read: not yet subpoenaed for questioning), whereas the osteologist tended to favour a dialogue, however cautious and clear-eyed, with the left. The newly elected secretary had been receiving telegrams and telephone calls of congratulation, even from the opposition. Cardamone, who in an interview appeared moved but determined, declared that he would commit himself to the best of his abilities not to betray his predecessor's hallowed memory, and concluded by asserting that he would devote 'his diligent labour and knowledge' to the now-renovated party.

'Thank God he'll devote it to the party,' Inspector Montalbano couldn't help but exclaim, since Dr Cardamone's knowledge, surgically speaking, had left more people hobbled than a violent earthquake usually does.

The newsman's next words made the inspector prick up his ears. To enable Cardamone to follow his own path without losing sight of the principles and people that represented the very best of Luparello's political endeavours, the members of the secretariat had besought Counsellor Pietro Rizzo, the engineer's spiritual heir, to work alongside the new secretary. After some understandable resistance, given the onerous tasks that came with the unexpected appointment, Rizzo had let himself be persuaded to accept. In his interview with Televigàta, Rizzo, also deeply moved, declared that he had no choice but to assume this weighty burden if he was to remain faithful to the memory of his mentor and friend, whose watchword was always and only: 'to serve'.

Montalbano reacted with surprise. How could this new secretary so blithely swallow having to work, with official sanction, alongside the man who had been his principal adversary's most loyal right-hand man? His surprise was short-lived, however, and proved naive once the inspector had given the matter a moment's rational thought. Indeed, that party had always distinguished itself by its innate inclination for compromise, for finding the middle path. It was possible that Cardamone didn't yet have enough clout to go it alone and felt the need for extra support.

He changed the channel. On the Free Channel, the voice of the leftist opposition, there was Nicolò Zito, the most influential of their editorialists, explaining how in Sicily, and in the province of Montelusa in particular, *mutatis mutandis* – or *zara zabara,* to say it in Sicilian – things never budged, even when there was a storm on the horizon. He quoted, with obvious facility, the prince of Salina's famous statement about changing everything in order to change nothing and concluded that Luparello and Cardamone were two sides of the same coin, the alloy that coin was made of being none other than Counsellor Rizzo.

Montalbano rushed to the phone, dialled the Free Channel's number, and asked for Zito. There was a bond of common sympathy, almost friendship, between him and the newsman.

'What can I do for you, Inspector?'

'I want to see you.'

'My dear friend, I'm leaving for Palermo tomorrow morning and will be away for at least a week. How about if I come by to see you in half an hour? And fix me something to eat. I'm starving.'

A dish of pasta with garlic and oil could be served up without any problem. He opened the refrigerator:

Adelina had prepared a hefty dish of boiled shrimp, enough for four. Adelina was the mother of a pair of repeat offenders, the younger of whom was still in prison, having been arrested by Montalbano himself three years earlier.

*

The previous July, when she had come to Vigàta to spend two weeks with him, Livia, upon hearing this story, became terrified.

'Are you insane? One of these days that woman will take revenge and poison your soup!'

'Take revenge for what?'

'For having arrested her son!'

'Is that my fault? Adelina's well aware it's not my fault if her son was stupid enough to get caught. I played fair, didn't use any tricks or traps to arrest him. It was all on the level.'

'I don't give a damn about your contorted way of thinking. You have to get rid of her.'

'But if I fire her, who's going to keep house for me, do my laundry, iron my clothes and make me dinner?'

'You'll find somebody else!'

'There you're wrong. I'll never find a woman as good as Adelina.'

*

He was about to put the pasta water on the stove when the telephone rang.

'I feel like crawling underground for waking you at this hour,' was the introduction.

'I wasn't sleeping. Who is this?'

'It's Counsellor Pietro Rizzo.'

'Ah, Counsellor Rizzo. My congratulations.'

'For what? If it's for the honour my party has just done me, you should probably offer me your condolences. Believe me, I accepted only out of a sense of undying loyalty to the ideals of the late Mr Luparello. But to get back to my reason for calling: I need to see you, Inspector.'

'Now?!'

'Not now, of course, but bear in mind, in any case, that it is an improcrastinable matter.'

'We could do it tomorrow morning, but isn't the funeral tomorrow? You'll be very busy, I imagine.'

'Indeed. All afternoon as well. There will be some

very important guests, you know, and of course they will linger awhile.'

'So when?'

'Actually, on second thoughts, I think we could do it tomorrow morning, but first thing. What time do you usually get to the office?'

'Around eight.'

'Eight o'clock would be fine with me. It will take but a few minutes.'

'Listen, Counsellor, precisely because you will have so little time tomorrow morning, could you perhaps tell me in advance what it's about?'

'Over the phone?'

'Just a hint.'

'All right. I have heard – though I don't know how much truth there is in the rumour – that an object found by chance on the ground was turned over to you. I've been instructed to reclaim it.'

Montalbano covered the receiver with one hand and literally exploded in a horselike whinny, a mighty guffaw. He had baited the Jacomuzzi hook with the necklace, and the trap had worked like a charm, catching the biggest fish he could ever have hoped for. But how did Jacomuzzi manage to let everyone know things he wasn't supposed to let anyone know? Did he resort to lasers, to telepathy, to magical shamanistic practices? Montalbano heard Rizzo yelling on the line.

'Hello? Hello? I can't hear you! What happened, did we get cut off?'

'No, excuse me, I dropped my pencil and was looking for it. I'll see you tomorrow at eight.'

*

As soon as he heard the doorbell ring, he put the pasta in the water and went to the door.

'So what's for supper?' asked Zito as he entered.

'Pasta with garlic and oil, and shrimp with oil and lemon.'

'Excellent.'

'Come into the kitchen and give me a hand. Meanwhile, my first question is: can you say "improcrastinable"?'

'Have you gone soft in the head? You make me race all the way from Montelusa to ask me if I can say some word? Anyway, of course I can say it. No problem.'

He tried to say it three or four times, with

increasing obstinacy, but he couldn't do it, getting more and more marble-mouthed with each try.

'You have to be very adroit, very adroit,' said the inspector, thinking of Rizzo, and he wasn't referring only to the lawyer's adroitness in casually uttering tongue-twisters.

As they ate, they spoke of eating, as always happens in Italy. Zito, after reminiscing about the heavenly shrimp he had enjoyed ten years earlier at Fiacca, criticized these for being a little overdone and regretted that they lacked a hint of parsley.

'So how is it that you've all turned British at the Free Channel?' Montalbano broke in without warning, as they were drinking an exquisite white wine his father had found near Randazzo. He had come by with six bottles the previous week, although they had been merely an excuse for them to spend a little time together.

'In what sense, British?'

'In the sense that you've refrained from dragging Luparello through the mud, as you would certainly have done in the past. Jesus Christ, the man dies of a heart attack in a kind of open-air brothel among whores, pimps and buggers, his trousers down around his ankles – it's downright obscene – and you guys, instead of seizing the moment for all it's worth, you all toe the line and cast a veil of mercy over how he died.'

'We're not really in the habit of taking advantage of such things.'

Montalbano started laughing.

'Would you do me a favour, Nicolò? Would you and everyone else at the Free Channel please go fuck yourselves?'

Zito started laughing in turn.

'All right, here's what happened. A few hours after the body was found, Counsellor Rizzo dashed over to see Baron Filò di Baucina, the "red baron", a millionaire but a communist, and begged him, with hands folded, not to let the Free Channel mention the circumstances of Luparello's death. He appealed to the sense of chivalry that the baron's ancestors seem, long ago, to have possessed. As you know, the baron owns eighty per cent of the network. Simple as that.'

'Simple as that, my arse. And so you, Nicolò Zito, who have won the admiration of your adversaries for always saying what needed to be said, you just say, "*Yes,* sir" to the baron and lie down?'

'What colour is my hair?' asked Zito by way of reply.

'It's red.'

'I'm red inside and out, Montalbano. I belong to the bad, rancorous communists, an endangered species. I accepted the whole bit because I was convinced that those who were saying we shouldn't sully the poor bastard's memory by dwelling on the circumstances of his death actually wished him ill, not well, as they were trying to make us think.'

'I don't understand.'

'Well, let me explain, my innocent friend. The quickest way to make people forget a scandal is to talk about it as much as possible, on television, in the papers, and so on. Over and over you flog the same dead horse, and pretty soon people start getting fed up. "They're really dragging this out!" they say. "Haven't we had enough?" After a couple of weeks the saturation effect is such that nobody wants to hear another word about that scandal. Now do you understand?'

'I think so.'

'If, on the other hand, you hush everything up, the silence itself starts to talk, rumours begin to multiply out of control until you can't stop them any more. You want an example? Do you know how many phone calls we've received at the studio precisely because of our silence? Hundreds. So is it true that Mr Luparello used to do two women at a time in his car? Is it true that Mr Luparello liked to do the sandwich, fucking a whore while a black man worked on him from behind? Then the latest, which came in tonight: is it true that Luparello used to give all his prostitutes fabulous jewels? Apparently somebody found one at the Pasture. Speaking of which, do you know anything about this story?'

'Me? No, that's just bullshit,' the inspector calmly lied.

'See? I'm sure that in a few months some arsehole will come to me and ask if it's true that Luparello used to bugger little four-year-olds and then stuff them with chestnuts and eat them. The slandering of his name will become eternal, the stuff of legend. That, I hope, will help you understand why I agreed to sweep it all under the carpet.'

'And what's Cardamone's position?'

'I don't know. That was very strange, his election. In the provincial secretariat they were all Luparello's men, you see, except for two, who were Cardamone's, but they were there just for the sake of appearances, to show that they were democratic and all. Clearly the new secretary could have been and should have been a follower of Luparello. Instead, surprise: Rizzo stands up and proposes Cardamone. The other members of the clique were speechless but didn't dare object. If Rizzo's talking this way, it must mean there's something lurking beneath all this which could turn dangerous; better follow the counsellor down that path. And so they vote in favour. Cardamone gets the call, accepts the post, and himself proposes that Rizzo work alongside him, to the great dismay of his two representatives in the secretariat. But here I understand Cardamone: better to have Rizzo aboard – he must have thought – than at large like a loose cannon.'

Zito then proceeded to tell him about a novel he was planning to write, and they went on till four.

*

As he was checking the health of a succulent plant, a gift from Livia that he kept on the windowsill in his office, Montalbano saw a blue government car pull up, the kind equipped with telephone, chauffeur and bodyguard, the latter of which got out first and opened the rear door for a short, bald man wearing a suit the same colour as the car.

'There's someone outside who needs to talk to me,' he said to the guard. 'Send him right in.'

When Rizzo entered, the inspector noted that the upper part of his left sleeve was covered by a broad black band the width of a palm: the counsellor was already in mourning for the funeral.

'What can I do to win your forgiveness?'

'For what?'

'For having disturbed you at home, at so late an hour.'

'But you said the matter was improcr—'

'Improcrastinable, yes.'

Such a clever man, Counsellor Pietro Rizzo!

'I'll come to the point. Late last Sunday night a young couple, highly respectable people, having had a bit to drink, decided to indulge an imprudent whim. The wife persuaded the husband to take her to the Pasture. She was curious about the place and what goes on there. A reprehensible curiosity, to be sure, but nothing more. When the pair arrived at the edge of the Pasture, the woman got out of the car.

But almost immediately people began to harass her with obscene propositions, so she got back in the car and they left. Back at home she realized she'd lost a precious object she was wearing around her neck.'

'What a strange coincidence,' muttered Montalbano, as if to himself.

'Excuse me?'

'I was just noting that at around the same time, and in the same place, Silvio Luparello was dying.'

Rizzo didn't lose his composure, but assumed a grave expression.

'I noticed the same thing, you know. Tricks of fate.'

'The object you mention, is it a solid-gold necklace with a heart studded with precious stones?'

'That's the one. I'm here to ask you to return it to its rightful owners, with the same discretion, of course, as you showed when my poor Mr Luparello was found dead.'

'You'll have to forgive me,' said the inspector, 'but I haven't the slightest idea of how to proceed in a case like this. In any event, I think it would have been a different story if the owner herself had come forward.'

'But I have a proper letter of attorney!'

'Really? Let me see it.'

'No problem, Inspector. You must understand that before bandying my clients' names about, I wanted to be quite sure you had the object they were looking for.'

He reached into his jacket pocket, extracted a sheet of paper, and handed it to Montalbano. The inspector read it carefully.

'Who's this Giacomo Cardamone that signed the letter?'

'He's the son of Dr Cardamone, our new provincial secretary.'

Montalbano decided it was time to repeat the performance.

'But it's so strange!' he mumbled again almost inaudibly, assuming an air of deep contemplation.

'I'm sorry, what did you say?'

Montalbano did not answer at once, letting the other stew a moment in his own juices.

'I was just thinking that in this whole affair, fate, as you say, is playing too many tricks on us.'

'In what sense, if you don't mind my asking?'

'In the sense that the son of the new party secretary happens to be in the same place at the same time as the old secretary at the moment of his death. Curious, don't you think?'

'Now that you bring it to my attention, yes. But I am certain there is not the slightest connection between the two matters, absolutely certain.'

'So am I,' said Montalbano, adding, 'I don't understand this signature next to Giacomo Cardamone's.'

'That's his wife's signature. She's Swedish. A rather reckless woman, frankly, who seems unable to adapt to our ways.'

'How much is the piece worth, in your opinion?'

'I'm no expert, but the owners said about eighty million lire.'

'Then here's what we'll do: later this morning I'm going to call my colleague Jacomuzzi – he's got the necklace at the moment – and have it sent back to me. Tomorrow morning I'll send it over to your office with one of my men.'

'I don't know how to thank you—'

Montalbano cut him off.

'And you will give my man a proper receipt.'

'But of course!'

'As well as a cheque for ten million lire – I've taken the liberty of rounding up the value of the necklace

– which would be the usual percentage due anyone who finds valuables or large sums of money.'

Rizzo absorbed the blow almost gracefully.

'That seems quite fair. To whom should I make it out?'

'To Baldassare Montaperto, one of the two street cleaners who found Luparello's body.'

The lawyer carefully wrote down the name.

NINE

Rizzo had no sooner finished closing the door than Montalbano already began dialling Nicolò Zito's home phone number. What the lawyer had just told him had set in motion a mechanism inside his brain that outwardly manifested itself in a frantic need to act. Zito's wife answered.

'My husband just walked out. He's on his way to Palermo.' Then she said, suddenly suspicious, 'But didn't he stay with you last night?'

'He certainly did, signora, but something of importance occurred to me just this morning.'

'Wait, maybe I can still get him. I'll try calling him on the intercom.'

A few minutes later he heard his friend's panting, then his voice, 'What do you want? Wasn't last night enough for you?'

'I need some information.'

'If you can make it brief.'

'I want to know everything – but really everything, even the most bizarre rumours – about Giacomo Cardamone and his wife, who seems to be Swedish.'

'No "seems" about it. She's a statuesque six-footer with tits and legs like you wouldn't believe. But if you really want to know everything, that would take time, which I haven't got right now. Listen, let's do this: I'm going to leave now. On the way I'll give it some thought, and as soon as I arrive I'll send you a fax.'

'Send a fax to police headquarters? Here we still use tom-toms and smoke signals!'

'I meant I'll send a fax for you to my Montelusa office. You can pass by later this morning, or around midday.'

*

Montalbano had to do something, so he went out of his office and into the sergeants' room.

'How's Tortorella doing?'

Fazio looked over at the desk of his absent colleague.

'I went to see him yesterday. They've apparently decided to release him from the hospital on Monday.'

'Do you know how to get inside the old factory?'

'When they built the enclosure wall after shutting it down, they put in a tiny little door, so small you have to bend down to pass through it, an iron door.'

'Who's got the key?'

'I don't know. I can find out.'

'Don't just find out. I want it before noon.'

He went back into his office and phoned Jacomuzzi, who let him wait a bit before deciding to answer.

'What's wrong, you got dysentery?'

'Cut it, Montalbano. What do you want?'

'What have you found on the necklace?'

'What do you think? Nothing. Actually, fingerprints, but there are so many of them and they're such a mess they're indecipherable. What should I do?'

'Send it back to me before the end of the day. Understood? Before the end of the day.'

He heard Fazio's irritated voice shout from the next room. 'Jesus Christ! Is it possible nobody knows who this Sicilchim belonged to? It must have some sort of bankruptcy trustee, some official custodian!'

And, as soon as he saw Montalbano enter, 'It'd probably be easier to get the keys to St Peter's.'

The inspector told him he was going out and wouldn't be gone more than two hours. When he returned, he wanted to find that key on his desk.

*

As soon as she saw him in the doorway, Montaperto's wife turned pale and put her hand over her heart.

'Oh my God! What is it? What happened?'

'Nothing that you should worry about. Actually, I have good news for you, believe it or not. Is your husband home?'

'Yes, he got off early today.'

The young woman sat him in the kitchen and went to call Saro, who had lain down in the bedroom at the baby's side, hoping to get him to close his eyes for just a little while.

'Sit down,' the inspector said to Saro when he appeared, 'and listen to me carefully. Where were you thinking of taking your son with the money you would have got from pawning the necklace?'

'To Belgium,' Saro promptly replied. 'My brother

lives there, and he said we could stay at his house for a while.'

'Have you got the money for the journey?'

'Scrimping and saving here and there, we've managed to put a little aside,' said the woman, without repressing a hint of pride in her voice. 'But it's only enough for the trip.'

'Excellent. Now I want you to go to the station, today, and buy the tickets. Actually, no, take the bus and go to Raccadali – is there a travel agency there?'

'Yes. But why go all the way to Raccadali?'

'I don't want anyone here in Vigàta to know what you're planning to do. While you're doing that, your wife should be packing for the journey. You mustn't tell anyone where you're going, not even family. Is that clear?'

'Perfectly clear, as far as that goes. But excuse me, Inspector, is there anything wrong in going to Belgium to have your son treated? You're telling me to do all these things on the sly, as if we were doing something illegal.'

'You're not doing anything illegal, Saro, no need to worry about that. But there are a lot of things I want to be absolutely sure about, so you'll have to trust me and do exactly as I say.'

'All right, but maybe you forgot. What are we going to Belgium for if the money we've got is barely enough to get us there and back? To go sightseeing?'

'You'll get the money you need. Tomorrow morning one of my men will bring you a cheque for ten million lire.'

'Ten million? What for?' asked Saro, breathless.

'You've earned it. It's the percentage you're entitled to for turning in the necklace you found. You can spend the money openly, without worry. As soon as you get the cheque, cash it immediately and then leave.'

'Who's the cheque from?'

'From Counsellor Rizzo.'

'Ah,' said Saro, turning pale.

'You mustn't be afraid. It's all legitimate, and in my hands. Still, it's best to be as careful as possible. I wouldn't want Rizzo to change his mind, out of the blue, like some bastards. Ten million lire, after all, is still ten million lire.'

*

Giallombardo told Montalbano that the sergeant had gone to get the key to the old factory but wouldn't be back for at least two hours; the custodian, who was not in good health, was staying with a son in Montedoro. The policeman also informed him that Judge Lo Bianco had phoned, looking for him, and wanted to be called back by ten o'clock.

*

'Ah, Inspector, excellent, I was just on my way out, I have to go to the cathedral for the funeral. And I know I will be assaulted, literally assaulted, by influential people all asking me the same question. Do you know what question that is?'

'Why hasn't the Luparello case been closed yet?'

'You guessed it, Inspector, and it's no joke. I don't want to use harsh words, and I don't want to be misunderstood in any way . . . but, in short, if you've got something concrete in hand, then out with it. Otherwise close the case. And let me say I simply don't understand: what do you think you're going to discover? Mr Luparello died of natural causes. And you, I have the impression, are digging your heels in only because he happened to die in the Pasture. I'm curious. If Luparello had been discovered at the side of the road, would you have found anything wrong with that? Answer me.'

'No.'

'So where do you want to go with this? The case must be closed by tomorrow. Understood?'

'Don't get angry, Judge.'

'Well, I am indeed angry, but only at myself. You're making me use a word, the word "case", that really should not properly be used in this case. By tomorrow, understood?'

'Could we make it Saturday?'

'What are we doing? Bartering at the market? All right. But if you are so much as an hour late, your superiors will hear about this.'

*

Zito kept his word, and the Free Channel office secretary handed him the fax from Palermo. Montalbano read it as he headed off to the Pasture.

> Young Mr Giacomo is a classic example of the spoiled rich kid, very true to the model, from which he hasn't the imagination to deviate. His father is

notoriously honourable, except for one peccadillo (more of which below), the opposite of the late lamented Luparello. Giacomino lives with his second wife, Ingrid Sjostrom, whose qualities I have already personally described to you, on the second floor of his father's villa. I shall now enumerate his exploits, at least those I can remember. An ignorant dolt, he never wanted to study or apply himself to anything other than the precocious analysis of pussy, but nevertheless he always passed with flying colours, thanks to the intervention of the Eternal Father (or more simply, his father). He never attended any university courses, though enrolled in the medical school (just as well for the public health). At age sixteen, driving his father's powerful car without a licence, he ran over and killed an eight-year-old boy. Giacomino, for all practical purposes, never paid for this, but the father did, and handsomely at that, compensating the child's family. As an adult he set up a business in services. Two years later the business failed, Cardamone lost not a penny, but his business partner nearly shot himself. A revenue officer trying to get to the bottom of things found himself suddenly transferred to Bolzano. Giacomino is currently in pharmaceuticals (imagine that! Daddy's the brains behind it, of course) and throws around a lot more money than he probably takes in.

An enthusiast for racing cars and horses, he has founded a polo club (in Montelusa!) where not a single game of that noble sport has ever been played, but there is plenty of snorting to make up for this lack.

If I had to express my sincere opinion of the man, I would say that he represents a splendid specimen of the nincompoop, of the sort that flourish wherever there is a rich and powerful father. At age twenty-two he contracted matrimony (isn't that how you say it?) with one Albamarina (Baba, to friends) Collatino, from a wealthy Palermo business family. Two years later Baba went to the Rota with a request for annulment, on the grounds of manifest *impotentia generandi* on the part of her spouse. I forgot to mention that at age eighteen, that is, four years before the marriage, Giacomino got one of the maids' daughters pregnant, and the regrettable incident was, as usual, hushed up by the Almighty. Thus there are two possibilities: either Baba was lying or the maid's daughter was lying. In the uncensurable opinion of the holy Roman prelates, it was the maid who had lied (how could it be otherwise?), and Giacomino was incapable of procreating (and for this we should thank the Lord in heaven). Granted her annulment, Baba got engaged to a cousin with whom she'd already had relations, while Giacomino headed toward the foggy lands of the north to forget.

In Sweden, he happened to attend a treacherous sort of rally race, the course of which ran around lakes, crags, and mountains. The winner was a tall, beautiful blonde, a mechanic by profession, whose name is, of course, Ingrid Sjostrom. How shall I put it, my friend, to avoid having it all sound like a soap opera? *Coup de foudre,* followed by marriage. They have now been living together for five years, and from time to time Ingrid goes back home and enters her little auto races. She cuckolds her husband with Swedish ease and simplicity. The other day at the polo club, five gentlemen (so to speak) played a party game. One of the questions asked was 'Will anyone who has not made it with Ingrid please stand?' All five remained seated. They all had a good laugh, especially Giacomino, who was present, though he didn't take part in the game. There is a rumour, totally unverifiable, that even the austere Dr Cardamone père has wet his whistle with his daughter-in-law. And this is the peccadillo I alluded to at the start. Nothing else comes to mind. I hope I've been enough of a gossip for your purposes. Vale –

NICOLÒ

Montalbano arrived at the Pasture about two. There wasn't a living soul around. The lock on the little iron door was encrusted with salt and rust. He had expected this and had expressly brought along the oil spray used to lubricate firearms. He went back to the car and turned on the radio, waiting for the oil to do its work.

The funeral – as a local radio announcer recounted – had reached some very high peaks of emotion, so that at one point the widow had felt faint and had to be carried outside. The eulogies were given, in order, by the bishop, the national vice-secretary of the party, the regional secretary, and, in a personal vein, by Minister Pellicano, who had long been a friend of the deceased. A crowd of at least two thousand people waited in front of the church for the casket to emerge, at which point they burst into warm, deeply touched applause.

'Warm' is fine, but how can applause be 'deeply touched'? Montalbano asked himself. He turned off the radio

and went to try the key. It turned in the lock, but the door seemed anchored to the ground. Pushing it with his shoulder, he finally managed to open it a crack, just wide enough to squeeze through. The door was obstructed by plaster chips, metal scraps, and sand; obviously the custodian hadn't been around for years. He noticed that there were actually two outer walls: the protective wall with the little entrance door and a crumbling old enclosure wall that had once surrounded the factory when it was running. Through the breaches in this second wall he could see rusted machinery, large tubes – some twisted, some straight – gigantic alembics, iron scaffolds with big holes, trestles hanging in absurd equilibrium, steel turrets soaring at illogical angles. And everywhere gashes in the flooring, great voids once covered with iron truss beams now broken and ready to fall below, where there was nothing any more except a layer of dilapidated cement with yellowing spikes of grass shooting up from the cracks. Montalbano stood motionless in the gap between the two walls, taking it all in, spellbound. While he liked the view of the factory from the outside, he was thrilled by the inside and regretted not having brought a camera. Then a low, continuous sound distracted his attention, a kind of sonic vibration that seemed to be coming, in fact, from inside the factory.

What machinery could be running in here? he asked himself, suspicious.

He thought it best to exit, return to his car, and get his pistol from the glove compartment. He hardly ever carried a weapon; the weight bothered him, and the gun rumpled his trousers and jackets. Going back inside the factory, where the noise continued, he began to walk carefully toward the side furthest from where he had entered. The drawing Saro had made was extremely precise and served as his guide. The noise was like the humming that certain high-tension wires sometimes make in very humid conditions, except that here the sound was more varied and musical and broke off from time to time, only to resume almost at once with a different modulation. He advanced, tense, taking care not to trip over the rocks and debris that constituted the floor in the narrow corridor between the two walls, when out of the corner of his eye, through an opening, he saw a man moving parallel to him inside the factory. He drew back, sure the other had already seen him. There was no time to lose; the man must have accomplices.

Montalbano leapt forward, weapon in hand, and shouted, 'Stop! Police!'

He realized in a fraction of a second that the other had anticipated this move and was already half bent forward, pistol in hand. Diving down, Montalbano pulled the trigger, and before he hit the ground, he managed to fire another two shots. But instead of hearing what he expected – a return shot, a cry, a shuffling of fleeing steps – he heard a deafening explosion and then a tinkling of glass breaking to pieces. When in an instant he realized what had happened, he was overcome by laughter so violent that he couldn't stand up. He had shot at himself, at the image that a large surviving pane of glass, tarnished and dirty, had cast back at him.

I can't tell anyone about this, he said to himself. *I would be asked to resign and ridden out of the force on a rail.*

The gun he was holding in his hand suddenly looked ridiculous to him, and he stuck it inside his belt. The shots, their long echo, the crash and the shattering of the glass had completely covered up the sound, which presently resumed, more varied than before. Now he understood: it was the wind, which every day, even in summer, lashed that stretch of beach, then abated in the evening, as if not wanting to disturb Gegè's business. Threading through the trestles' metal cables – some of them broken, some of them taut – and through smokestacks pocked with holes like giant flutes, the wind played its plaintive melody inside the dead factory, and the inspector paused, entranced, to listen.

It took him almost half an hour to reach the spot that Saro had indicated, having had, at various points, to climb over piles of debris. At last he figured he was exactly parallel to the spot where Saro had found the necklace on the other side of the wall, and he started looking calmly around. Magazines and scraps of paper yellowed by sun, weeds, Coca-Cola bottles (the cans being too light to be thrown over the high wall), wine bottles, a bottomless metal wheelbarrow, a few tyres, some iron scraps, an unidentifiable object, a rotten wooden beam. And beside the beam a leather handbag with strap, stylish, brand-new, stamped with a designer name. It clashed visibly with the surrounding ruin. Montalbano opened it. Inside were two rather large stones, apparently inserted as ballast to allow the bag to achieve the proper trajectory from outside the wall to inside, and nothing else. He took a closer look at the bag. The owner's metal initials had been torn off, but the leather still bore their impressions, an *I* and an *S*: Ingrid Sjostrom.

They're serving it up to me on a silver platter, thought Montalbano.

TEN

The thought of accepting the platter so kindly being offered him, along with everything that might be on it, came to mind as he was refortifying himself with a generous helping of the roast peppers that Adelina had left in the refrigerator. He looked for Giacomo Cardamone's telephone number in the directory; his Swedish wife would probably be home at this hour.

'Who dat speakin'?'

'It's Giovanni. Is Ingrid there?'

'I go see, you wait.'

He tried to guess from what part of the world this housekeeper had landed in the Cardamone home, but he couldn't figure it out.

'Ciao, monster cock, how are you?'

It was a deep, husky voice, which fit the description Zito had given him. Her words, however, had no erotic effect whatsoever on the inspector. Actually, they made him feel upset: of all the names in the world, he had to go and pick one belonging to a man Ingrid knew down to his anatomical proportions.

'Are you still there? Did you fall asleep on your feet? Did you fuck a lot last night, you pig?'

'Excuse me, signora . . .'

Ingrid's reaction was immediate, an acceptance without surprise or indignation.

'You're not Giovanni.'

'No.'

'Then who are you?'

'I'm an inspector with the police force. My name is Montalbano.'

He expected an expression of alarm but was promptly disappointed.

'Ooh, how exciting! A cop! What do you want from me?'

Her tone remained familiar, even after she knew she was speaking with someone she didn't know. Montalbano maintained his formality.

'I would like to have a few words with you.'

'I can't this afternoon, but I'm free this evening.'

'All right then, this evening.'

'Where? Shall I come to your office? Tell me where it is.'

'Better not. I'd prefer somewhere more discreet.'

Ingrid paused.

'How about your bedroom?' The woman's voice had grown irritated. Apparently she was beginning to think that the person on the line was some imbecile trying to make advances.

'Listen, signora, I realize you're suspicious, with good reason. Let's do this: I'll be back at headquarters in Vigàta in an hour. You can phone there and ask for me. All right?'

The woman didn't answer immediately. She was thinking it over before making up her mind.

'No, I believe you, cop. Tell me when and where.'

They agreed on the place, the Marinella Bar, which at the appointed hour, ten o'clock, would surely be deserted. Montalbano advised her not to tell anyone, not even her husband.

*

The Luparello villa stood at the entry to Montelusa as one approached from the sea. A massive nineteenth-century building, it was surrounded by a high defensive wall with a wrought-iron gate at the centre, now thrown open. Montalbano walked down the tree-lined lane cutting through one part of the park and came to the huge, double front door, one half of which was open, the other half draped with a large black bow. He leaned forward to look inside: in the vestibule, which was rather vast, there were some twenty people, men and women, looking appropriately grief-stricken, murmuring in soft voices. He thought it unwise to walk through the crowd; someone might recognize him and start wondering why he was there. Instead, he walked all around the villa and at last found a rear entrance, which was closed. He rang the bell several times before someone came and opened the door.

'You've made a mistake. For condolence visits use the front door,' said a small, alert housekeeper in black pinafore and starched cap, who had classified him at a glance as not belonging to the category of caterers.

'I'm Inspector Montalbano. Could you tell one of the family I'm here?'

'They've been expecting you, Inspector.'

She led him down a long corridor, opened a door, and gestured for him to enter. Montalbano found himself in a large library with thousands of well-kept books neatly arrayed on enormous shelves. There was an immense desk in one corner, and in the corner opposite, a tastefully elegant sitting area with a small table and two armchairs. Only five paintings adorned the walls, and with a shudder of excitement Montalbano immediately recognized the artists: there was a Guttuso portrait of a peasant from the forties, a landscape in Lazio by Melli, a demolition by Mafai, two rowers on the Tiber by Donghi, and a woman bathing by Fausto Pirandello. The selection showed exquisite taste and rare discernment. The door opened, and a man of about thirty appeared: black tie, open face, stylish.

'It was I who phoned you. Thank you for coming. Mama was very keen on seeing you. I'm sorry for all the trouble I've caused you.' He spoke with no regional inflection whatsoever.

'No trouble at all. I simply don't see of what use I could be to your mother.'

'That's what I said to her, too, but she insisted. And she wouldn't give me any hint as to why she wished to inconvenience you.'

He looked at the fingertips of his right hand as if

seeing them for the first time, then discreetly cleared his throat.

'Please try to understand, Inspector.'

'I don't understand.'

'For Mama's sake. It's been a very trying time for her.'

The young man turned to leave, then suddenly stopped.

'Ah, Inspector, I wanted to inform you so you wouldn't find yourself in an embarrassing situation that Mama knows how my father died and where he died. How she found out, I have no idea. She already knew two hours after the body was found. Please excuse me.'

Montalbano felt relieved. If the widow knew, he wouldn't be forced to concoct any pious fictions to hide the indecency of her husband's death from her. He went back to enjoying the paintings. At his house in Vigàta he had only drawings and prints by Carmassi, Attardi, Guida, Cordio and Angelo Canevari, to which he had been able to treat himself by docking his meagre salary. More than that he couldn't afford; he could never pay for a painting on the level of these.

'Do you like them?'

He turned about abruptly. He hadn't heard the signora enter. She was a woman past fifty, not tall, with an air of determination; the tiny wrinkles lining her face had not yet succeeded in destroying the beauty of her features. On the contrary, they highlighted the radiance of her penetrating green eyes.

'Please make yourself comfortable,' she said, then went and sat on the sofa as the inspector took a seat in an armchair. 'Such beautiful pictures. I don't know much about painting, but I do like them. There are about thirty scattered around the house. My husband bought them. Painting was his secret vice, he loved to say. Unfortunately, it wasn't his only one.'

We're off to a good start, Montalbano thought, then asked, 'Are you feeling better, signora?'

'Compared to when?'

The inspector stammered, as if he were in front of a teacher asking him difficult questions.

'Well, I – I don't know, compared to this morning . . . I heard you were unwell today – in the cathedral.'

'Unwell? I was fine, as good as one might feel in such circumstances. No, my friend, I merely pretended to faint. I'm a good actress. Actually, a thought had come into my mind: if a terrorist, I said to myself, were to blow up this church with all of us inside, at least one-tenth of all the hypocrisy in the world would disappear with us. So I had myself escorted out.'

Impressed by the woman's candour, Montalbano didn't know what to say, so he waited for her to resume speaking.

'When I was told where my husband had been found, I called the police commissioner and asked him who was in charge of the investigation – if there *was* any investigation. The commissioner gave me your name, adding that you were a decent man. I had my doubts: *are* there still any decent men? And so I had my son phone you.'

'I can only thank you, signora.'

'But we're not here to exchange compliments. I don't want to waste your time. Are you absolutely certain it wasn't a homicide?'

'Absolutely.'

'Then what are your misgivings?'

'Misgivings?'

'Yes, my dear, you must have some. There is no other way to explain your reluctance to close the investigation.'

'I'll be frank, signora. They're only impressions,

impressions I really can't and shouldn't allow myself, in the sense that, since we are dealing with a death by natural causes, my duty should lie elsewhere. If you have nothing new to tell me, I shall inform the judge this very evening—'

'But I do have something new to tell you.'

Montalbano was struck dumb.

'I don't know what your impressions may be,' the signora continued, 'but I'll tell you what mine are. Silvio was, of course, a shrewd, ambitious man. If he stayed in the shadows all those years, it was with a specific purpose in mind: to come into the limelight at the right moment and stay there. Now, do you really believe that this man, after all that time spent on patient manoeuvres to get where he did, would decide, one fine evening, to go with a woman, surely of ill repute, to a shady place where anyone could recognize him and possibly blackmail him?'

'That, signora, is one of the things that has perplexed me the most.'

'Do you want to be even more perplexed? I said "woman of ill repute", and I would like to clarify that I didn't mean a prostitute or any sort of woman for whom one pays. I'm not sure if I'm explaining myself clearly. Let me tell you something: right after we got married, Silvio confided in me that he had never been with a prostitute or gone to a licensed brothel when they still existed. Something prevented him. So this leads one to wonder what sort of woman it was who convinced him to have relations with her in that hideous place.'

Montalbano had never been with a prostitute either, and he hoped that no new revelations about Luparello would reveal other points of similarity between him and a man with whom he would not have wanted to break bread.

'You see, my husband quite comfortably gave in to his vices, but he was never tempted by self-destruction, by that "ecstasy for baseness", as one French writer put it. He consummated his affairs discreetly, in a little house he had built, though not in his name, at the tip of Capo Massaria. I found out about it from the customary compassionate friend.'

She stood up, went over to the desk, rummaged through a drawer, then sat back down holding a large yellow envelope, a metal ring with two keys, and a magnifying glass. She handed the keys to the inspector.

'Incidentally, he had a mania for keys. He had two

copies of each set, one of which he would keep in that drawer; the other he always carried on his person. Well, the second copy was never found.'

'They weren't in your husband's pockets?'

'No. And they weren't in his engineering studio either. Nor were they found in his other office, the so-called political office. Vanished, evaporated.'

'He could have lost them on the street. We don't necessarily know that they were removed from him.'

'It's not possible. You see, my husband had six sets of keys. One for this house, one for the country house, one for the house by the sea, one for the office, one for the studio, one for his little house. He kept them all in the glove compartment of his car. From time to time he would take out the set he needed.'

'And none of these sets was found?'

'No. I gave orders to have all the locks changed. With the exception of the little house, of whose existence I am officially unaware. If you wish, you may visit the place. I'm sure you'll find some revealing vestiges of his affairs.'

Twice she had said 'his affairs', and Montalbano wished he could console her in some way.

'Aside from the fact that Mr Luparello's affairs do

not fall within the scope of my investigation, I have nevertheless questioned some people, and I must say in all sincerity that the answers I've received have been rather generic, applicable to anyone.'

The woman looked at him with the faint hint of a smile.

'I never did reproach him for it, you know. Practically speaking, two years after the birth of our son, my husband and I ceased to be a couple. And so I was able to observe him calmly and quietly for thirty years, without having my vision clouded by the agitation of the senses. You seem not to understand, please forgive me: in speaking of his "affairs", my intention was to avoid specifying the sex.'

Montalbano hunched his shoulders, sinking farther down into the armchair. He felt as if he'd just taken a blow to the head from a crowbar.

'On the other hand,' the woman continued, 'to get back to the subject of greatest interest to me, I am convinced that we are dealing with a criminal act – let me finish – not a homicide, not a physical elimination, but a political crime. An act of extreme violence was done, and it led to his death.'

'Please explain, signora.'

'I am convinced that my husband was forced, under the threat of violence or blackmail, to go to that disgraceful place where he was found. They had a plan, but they were unable to execute it in full because his heart gave out under the stress or – why not? – out of fear. He was very ill, you know. He had just been through a very difficult operation.'

'But how would they have forced him?'

'I don't know. Perhaps you can help me find out. They probably lured him into a trap. He was unable to resist. I don't know, maybe they photographed him at that place or had him recognized by someone. And from that moment on they had my husband in the palm of their hands; he became their puppet.'

'Who are "they"?'

'His political adversaries, I think, or some business associates.'

'You see, signora, your reasoning, or rather your conjecture, has one serious flaw: you have no proof to support it.'

The woman opened the yellow envelope she'd been holding in her hand all this time and pulled out some photographs, the ones the lab had taken of the corpse at the Pasture.

'Oh, God,' Montalbano murmured, shuddering. The woman, for her part, showed no emotion as she studied them.

'How did you get these?'

'I have good friends. Have you looked at them?'

'No.'

'You were wrong not to.' She chose a photo and handed it to Montalbano along with the magnifying glass. 'Now, take a good look at this one. His trousers are pulled down, and you can just get a glimpse of the white of his underpants.'

Montalbano was covered in sweat; the discomfort he felt irritated him, but there was nothing he could do about it.

'I don't see anything strange about that.'

'Oh, no? What about the label of the underpants?'

'Yes, I can see it. So?'

'You shouldn't be able to see it. This kind of brief – and if you come into my husband's bedroom, I'll show you others – has the label on the back and on the inside. If you can see them, as you can, it means they were put on backwards. And you can't tell me that Silvio when getting dressed that morning put them on that way and never noticed. He took a diuretic, you see, and had to go to the bathroom many times a day and could have easily put them properly back on at any point of the day. And this can mean only one thing.'

'What's that?' the inspector asked, stunned by the woman's lucid, pitiless analysis, which she made without shedding a tear, as though the deceased were a casual acquaintance.

'That he was naked when they surprised him, and that they forced him to get dressed in a hurry. And the only place he could have been naked was in the little house at Capo Massaria. That is why I gave you the keys. I repeat, it was a criminal act against my husband's public image, but only half successful. They wanted to make him out to be a pig, so they could feed him to the pigs at any moment. It would have been better if he hadn't died; forced to cover himself, he would have done whatever they asked. The plan did, however, succeed in part: all my husband's men have been excluded from the new leadership. Rizzo alone escaped; actually, he gained by it.'

'And why did he?'

'That is up to you to discover, if you so desire.

Or else you can stop at the shape they've given the water.'

'I'm sorry, I don't understand.'

'I'm not Sicilian; I was born in Grosseto and came to Montelusa when my father was made prefect here. We owned a small piece of land and a house on the slopes of the Amiata and used to spend our summers there. I had a little friend, a peasant boy, who was younger than me. I was about ten. One day I saw that my friend had put a bowl, a cup, a teapot and a square milk carton on the edge of a well, had filled them all with water, and was looking at them attentively.

' "What are you doing?" I asked him. And he answered me with a question in turn.

' "What shape is water?"

' "Water doesn't have any shape!" I said, laughing. "It takes the shape you give it." '

At that moment the door to the library opened, and an angel appeared.

ELEVEN

The angel – Montalbano at that moment didn't know how else to define him – was a young man of about twenty, tall, blond, very tanned, with a perfect body and an ephebic aura. A pandering ray of sun had taken care to bathe him in light in the doorway, accentuating the Apollonian features of his face.

'May I come in, *zia*?'

'Come in, Giorgio, come in.'

While the youth moved toward the sofa, weightlessly, his feet seeming not to touch the ground but merely to glide across the floor, navigating a sinuous, almost spiral path, brushing past objects within reach or, more than brushing, lightly caressing them, Montalbano caught a glance from the signora that told him to put the photograph he was holding in his pocket. He obeyed, while the widow quickly put the other photos back in the yellow envelope, which she placed beside her on the sofa. When the young man came near, the inspector noticed that his blue eyes were streaked with red, puffy from tears, and ringed with dark circles.

'How do you feel, *zia*?' he asked in an almost singing voice, then knelt elegantly beside the woman, resting his head in her lap. In Montalbano's mind flashed the memory, bright as if under a floodlight, of a painting he had seen once – he couldn't remember where – a portrait of an English lady with a greyhound in the exact same position as the one the young man had assumed.

'This is Giorgio,' the woman said. 'Giorgio Zìcari, son of my sister Elisabetta and Ernesto Zìcari, the criminal lawyer. Perhaps you know him.'

As she spoke, the woman caressed his hair. Giorgio gave no indication of having understood what was said. Visibly absorbed in his devastating grief, he didn't even bother to turn toward the inspector. The woman, moreover, had taken care not to tell her nephew who Montalbano was and what he was doing in their house.

'Were you able to sleep last night?'

Giorgio's only reply was to shake his head.

'I'll tell you what you should do. Did you notice that Dr Capuano's here? Go talk to him, have him prescribe you a strong sedative, then go back to bed.'

Without a word, Giorgio stood up fluidly, levitated over the floor with his curious, spiral manner of movement, and disappeared beyond the door.

'You must forgive him,' the lady said. 'Giorgio is without doubt the one who has suffered most, and who suffers most, from the death of my husband. You see, I wanted my own son to study and find himself a position independently of his father, far from Sicily. You can perhaps imagine my reasons for this. As a result, in Stefano's absence my husband poured all his affection on our nephew, and his love was returned to the point of idolatry. The boy even came to live with us, to the great displeasure of my sister and her husband, who felt abandoned.'

She stood up, and Montalbano did likewise.

'I've told you everything I thought I should tell you, Inspector. I know I'm in honest hands. You may call me whenever you see fit, at any hour of the day or night. And don't bother to spare my feelings; I'm what they call "a strong woman". In any event, act as your conscience dictates.'

'One question, signora, which has been troubling me for some time. Why weren't you concerned to make it known that your husband hadn't returned . . .? What I mean is, wasn't it disturbing that your husband didn't come home that night? Had it happened before?'

'Yes, it had. But, you see, he phoned me on Sunday night.'

'From where?'

'I couldn't say. He said he would be home very late. He had an important meeting and might even be forced to spend the night away.'

She extended her hand to him, and the inspector, without knowing why, squeezed it in his own and then kissed it.

*

Once outside, having exited by the same rear door of the villa, he noticed Giorgio sitting on a stone bench nearby, bent over, shuddering convulsively.

Concerned, Montalbano approached and saw the youth's hands open and drop the yellow envelope and the photos, which scattered about on the ground. Apparently, spurred by a catlike curiosity, he had got hold of them when crouching beside his aunt.

'Are you unwell?'

'Not like that, oh, God, not like that!'

Giorgio spoke in a clotted voice, his eyes glassy, and hadn't even noticed the inspector standing there. It took a second, then suddenly he stiffened, falling backwards from the bench, which had no back. Montalbano knelt beside him, trying in some way to immobilize that spasm-racked body; a white froth was beginning to form at the corners of the boy's mouth.

Stefano Luparello appeared at the door to the villa, looked around, saw the scene, and came running.

'I was coming after you to say hello. What's happening?'

'An epileptic fit, I think.'

They did their best to prevent Giorgio, at the height of the crisis, from biting off his tongue or striking his head violently against the ground. Then the youth calmed down, his shudders diminishing in fury.

'Help me carry him inside,' said Stefano.

The same maid who had opened the door for the inspector came running at Stefano's first call.

'I don't want Mama to see him in this state.'

'My room,' said the girl.

They walked with difficulty down a different corridor from the one the inspector had taken upon entering. Montalbano held Giorgio by the armpits, with Stefano grabbing the feet. When they arrived in the servants' wing, the maid opened a door. Panting, they laid the boy down on the bed. Giorgio had plunged into a leaden sleep.

'Help me to undress him,' said Stefano.

Only when the youth was stripped down to his boxers and T-shirt did Montalbano notice that from the base of the neck up to the bottom of his chin, the skin was extremely white, diaphanous, in sharp contrast to the face and the chest, which were bronzed by the sun.

'Do you know why he's not tanned there?' he asked Stefano.

'I don't know,' he said. 'I got back to Montelusa just last Monday afternoon, after being away for months.'

'I know why,' said the maid. 'Master Giorgio hurt himself in a car accident. He took the collar off less than a week ago.'

'When he comes to and can understand,' Montalbano said to Stefano, 'tell him to drop by my office in Vigàta tomorrow morning, around ten.'

He went back to the bench, bent down to the ground to pick up the envelope and photos, which Stefano had not noticed, and put them in his pocket.

*

Capo Massaria was about a hundred yards past the San Filippo bend, but the inspector couldn't see the little house that supposedly stood right on the point, at least according to what Signora Luparello had told him. He started to back the car up, proceeding very slowly. When he was exactly opposite the cape, he espied, amid dense, low trees, a path forking off the main road. He took this and shortly afterwards found the small road blocked by a gate, the sole opening in a long dry-stone wall that sealed off the part of the cape that jutted out over the sea.

The keys were the right ones. Leaving the car outside the gate, Montalbano headed up a garden path made of blocks of tufa set in the ground. At the end of this he went down a small staircase, also made of tufa, which led to a sort of landing where he found the house's front door, invisible from the landward side because it was built like an eagle's nest, right into the rock, similar to a mountain refuge.

Entering, he found himself inside a vast room facing the sea, indeed suspended over the sea, and the impression of being on a ship's deck was reinforced by an entire wall of glass. The place was in perfect order. There was a dining table with four chairs in one corner, a sofa and two armchairs turned toward the window, a nineteenth-century sideboard full of glasses, dishes, bottles of wine and liqueur, and a television with a VCR. On top of a low table beside it was a row of video cassettes, some pornographic, others not. The large room had three doors, the first of which opened onto an immaculate kitchenette with shelves packed with foodstuffs and a refrigerator almost empty except for a few bottles of champagne and vodka. The bathroom, which was quite spacious, smelled of disinfectant. On the shelf under the mirror were an electric razor, deodorants and a flask of eau de cologne. In the bedroom, which also had a large window looking onto the sea, there was a double bed covered with a freshly laundered sheet; two bedside tables, one with a telephone; and a wardrobe with three doors. On the wall at the head of the bed, a drawing by Emilio Greco, a very sensual nude. Montalbano opened the drawer of the bedside table with the telephone, no doubt the side of the bed Luparello usually slept on. Three condoms, a pen, a white notepad. He gave a start when he saw the pistol, a 7.65, at the very back of the drawer, loaded. The drawer to the other bedside table was empty. Opening the left-hand door of the wardrobe, he saw two men's suits. In the top drawer, a shirt, three sets of underpants, some handkerchiefs, a T-shirt. He checked the underpants: the signora was right, the label was inside and in the back. In the bottom drawer, a pair of loafers and a pair of slippers. The wardrobe's middle door was covered by a mirror that reflected the bed. That section was divided into three shelves: the topmost and middle shelves contained, jumbled together, hats, Italian and foreign magazines whose common denominator was pornography, a vibrator, sheets and pillowcases. On the bottom shelf were three female wigs on their respective stands – one brown, one blonde, one red. Maybe they were part of the engineer's erotic games. The biggest surprise, however, came when he opened the right-hand door: two women's dresses, very elegant, on coat hangers. There were also two pairs of jeans and some blouses. In a drawer, minuscule panties but no bras. The other was empty. As he leaned forward to better inspect this second drawer, Montalbano understood what it was that had so surprised him: not the sight of the feminine apparel but the scent that emanated from them, the very same he had smelled, only more vaguely, at the old factory, the moment he'd opened the leather handbag.

There was nothing else to see. Just to be thorough, he bent down to look under the furniture. A tie had been wrapped around one of the rear legs of the bed. He picked it up, remembering that Luparello had been found with his shirt collar unbuttoned. He took the photographs out of his pocket and decided that the tie, for its colour, would have gone quite well with the suit the engineer was wearing at the time of his death.

*

At headquarters he found Germanà and Galluzzo in a state of agitation.

'Where's the sergeant?'

'Fazio's with the others at a petrol station, the one on the way to Marinella. There was some shooting there.'

'I'll go there at once. Did anything come for me?'

'Yes, a package from Jacomuzzi.'

He opened it. It was the necklace. He wrapped it back up.

'Germanà, you come with me to this petrol station. You'll drop me off there and continue on to Montelusa in my car. I'll tell you what road to take.'

He went into his office, phoned Rizzo, told him the necklace was on its way with one of his men, and added that he should hand over the cheque for ten million lire to the agent.

As they were heading toward the site of the shooting, the inspector explained to Germanà that he must not turn the package over to Rizzo before he had the cheque in his pocket and that he was to take this cheque – he gave him the address – to Saro Montaperto, advising him to cash it as soon as the bank opened, at eight o'clock the following morning. He couldn't say why, and this bothered him a great deal, but he sensed that the Luparello affair was quickly drawing to a conclusion.

'Should I come back and pick you up at the petrol station?'

'No, stop at headquarters. I'll return in a squad car.'

*

The police car and a private vehicle were blocking the entrances to the petrol station. As soon as he stepped out of his car, with Germanà taking the road for Montelusa, the inspector was overwhelmed by the strong odour of petrol.

'Watch where you step!' Fazio shouted at him.

The gasoline had formed a kind of bog, the fumes of which made Montalbano feel nauseous and mildly faint. Stopped in front of the station was a car with a Palermo licence plate, its windscreen shattered.

'One person was injured, the guy at the wheel,' said the sergeant. 'He was taken away by ambulance.'

'Seriously injured?'

'No, just a scratch. But it scared him to death.'

'What happened, exactly?'

'If you want to speak to the station attendant yourself . . .'

The man answered Montalbano's questions in a voice so high pitched that it had the same effect on him as fingernails on glass. Things had happened more or less as follows: a car had stopped, the only person inside had asked him to fill it up, the attendant had stuck the nozzle into the car and left it there to do its work, setting it on automatic stop because meanwhile another car had pulled in and its driver had asked for thirty thousand in gas and a quick oil check. As the attendant was about to serve the second client, a car on the road had fired a burst from a sub-machine gun and sped off, disappearing in traffic. The man at the wheel of the first car had set off immediately in pursuit, the nozzle had slipped out and continued to pump gasoline. The driver of the second vehicle was shouting like a madman; his shoulder had been grazed by a bullet. Once the initial moment of panic had passed and he realized there was no more danger, the attendant had assisted the injured man, while the pump continued to spread gasoline all over the ground.

'Did you get a good look at the face of the man in the first car, the one that drove off in pursuit?'

'No, sir.'

'Are you really sure?'

'As sure as there's a God in heaven.'

Meanwhile, the firemen summoned by Fazio arrived.

'Here's what we'll do,' Montalbano said to the sergeant. 'As soon as the firemen are done, pick up the attendant, who hasn't convinced me one bit, and take him down to the station. Put some pressure on him: the guy knows perfectly well who the man they shot at was.'

'I think so, too.'

'How much do you want to bet it's one of the Cuffaro gang? I think this month it's their turn to get it.'

'What, you want to take the money right out of my pocket?' the sergeant asked, laughing. 'That's a bet you've already won.'

'See you later.'

'Where are you going? I thought you wanted me to give you a lift in the squad car.'

'I'm going home to change my clothes. It's only about twenty minutes from here on foot. A little breath of air will do me good.'

He headed off. He didn't feel like meeting Ingrid Sjostrom dressed in his Sunday best.

TWELVE

He plonked down in front of the television right out of the shower, still naked and dripping. The images were from Luparello's funeral that morning, and the cameraman had apparently realized that the only people capable of lending a sense of drama to the ceremony – in every other way so like countless other tedious official events – were the trio of the widow, Stefano the son, and Giorgio the nephew. From time to time Signora Luparello, without realizing it, would jerk her head backwards, as if repeatedly saying no. This 'no' was interpreted by the commentator, in a low, sorrowful voice, as the obvious gesture of a creature irrationally rejecting the concrete fact of death; but as the cameraman was zooming in on her to catch the expression in her gaze, Montalbano found confirmation of what the widow had already confessed to him: there was only disdain and boredom in those eyes. Beside her sat her son, 'numb with grief', according to the announcer, and he called him 'numb' only because the composure the young engineer showed seemed to border on indifference. Giorgio instead teetered like a tree in the wind, livid as he swayed, continually twisting a tear-soaked handkerchief in his hands.

The telephone rang, and Montalbano went to answer it without taking his eyes off the television screen.

'Inspector, this is Germanà. Everything's been taken care of. Counsellor Rizzo expressed his thanks and said he'd find a way to repay you.'

Some of Rizzo's ways of repaying debts, he whispered to himself, his creditors would have gladly done without.

'Then I went to see Saro and gave him the cheque. It took some effort to convince them – they thought it was some kind of practical joke – and then they started kissing my hands. I'll spare you all the things they said the Lord should do for you. The car's at headquarters. You want me to bring it to you?'

The inspector glanced at his watch; there was still

a little more than an hour before his rendezvous with Ingrid.

'All right, but there's no hurry. Let's say nine-thirty. Then I'll give you a ride back into town.'

He didn't want to miss the moment when she pretended to faint. He felt like a spectator to whom the magician had revealed his secret: the pleasure would be in appreciating not the surprise but the skill. The one who missed it, however, was the cameraman, who was unable to capture that moment even though he had quickly panned from his close-up of the minister back to the group of family members, where Stefano and two volunteers were already carrying the signora out while Giorgio remained in place, still swaying.

*

Instead of dropping Germanà off in front of police headquarters and continuing on, Montalbano got out with him. Fazio was back from Montelusa, and he had spoken with the wounded man, who had finally calmed down. The man, the sergeant recounted, was a household-appliance salesman from Milan who every three months would catch a plane, land in Palermo, rent a car and drive around. Having stopped at the petrol station, he was looking at a piece of paper to check the address of the next store on his list of clients when he suddenly heard the shots and felt a sharp pain in his shoulder. Fazio believed his story.

'Chief, when this guy goes back to Milan, he's going to join up with the people who want to separate Sicily from the rest of Italy.'

'What about the attendant?'

'The attendant's another matter. Giallombardo's talking to him now, and you know what he's like: someone spends a couple of hours with him, talking like he's known him for a hundred years, and afterward he realizes he's told him secrets he wouldn't even tell the priest at confession.'

*

The lights were off, the glass entrance door barred shut. Montalbano had chosen the Marinella Bar on the one day it was closed. He parked the car and waited. A few minutes later a two-seater arrived, red and flat as a fillet of sole. The door opened, and Ingrid emerged. Even by the dim light of a street lamp, the inspector saw that she was even better than he had imagined her: tight jeans wrapping very long legs, white shirt open at the collar with the sleeves rolled up, sandals, hair gathered in a bun. A real cover girl. Ingrid looked around, noticed the darkness inside the bar, walked lazily but surely over to the inspector's car, then leaned forward to speak to him through the open window.

'See, I was right. So where do we go now? Your place?'

'No,' Montalbano said angrily. 'Get in.' The woman obeyed, and at once the car was filled with the scent that Montalbano already knew well.

'Where do we go now?' Ingrid repeated. She wasn't joking any more; utter female that she was, she had noticed the man's agitation.

'Do you have much time?'

'As much as I want.'

'We're going somewhere you'll feel comfortable, since you've already been there. You'll see.'

'What about my car?'

'We'll come back for it later.'

They set off, and after a few minutes of silence Ingrid asked him a question she should have asked from the start.

'Why did you want to see me?'

The inspector was mulling over the idea that had come to him as he told her to get in the car: it was a real cop's sort of idea, but he was, after all, a cop.

'I wanted to see you, Mrs Cardamone, because I need to ask you some questions.'

'Mrs Cardamone? Listen, Inspector, I'm very familiar with everyone I meet, and if you're too formal with me I'll only feel uncomfortable. What's your first name?'

'Salvo. Did Counsellor Rizzo tell you we found the necklace?'

'What necklace?'

'What do you mean, what necklace? The one with the diamond-studded heart.'

'No, he didn't tell me. Anyway, I have no dealings with him. He certainly must have told my husband.'

'Tell me something, I'm curious: are you in the habit of losing jewellery and then finding it again?'

'Why do you ask?'

'Come on, I tell you we found your necklace, which is worth about a hundred million lire, and you don't bat an eyelash?'

Ingrid gave a subdued laugh, confined to her throat.

'The fact is, I don't like jewellery. See?'

She showed him her hands.

'I don't wear rings, not even a wedding band.'

'Where did you lose the necklace?'

Ingrid didn't answer at once.

She's reviewing her lesson, thought Montalbano.

Then the woman began speaking, mechanically. Being a foreigner didn't help her to lie.

'I was curious about this place called the Pastor—'

'Pasture,' Montalbano corrected.

'I'd heard so much about it. I talked my husband into taking me there. Once there I got out, walked a little, and was almost attacked. I got scared and was afraid my husband would get in a fight. We left. Back at home I realized I no longer had the necklace on.'

'How did you happen to put it on that evening, since you don't like jewellery? It doesn't really seem appropriate for going to the Pasture.'

Ingrid hesitated.

'I had it on because that afternoon I'd been with a friend who wanted to see it.'

'Listen,' said Montalbano, 'I should preface all this by saying that even though I am, of course, talking to you as a police inspector, I'm doing so in an unofficial capacity.'

'What do you mean? I don't understand.'

'What I mean is, anything you tell me will remain between you and me. How did your husband happen to choose Rizzo as his lawyer?'

'Was he not supposed to?'

'No, at least not logically. Rizzo was the right-hand man of Silvio Luparello, who was your father-in-law's biggest political adversary. By the way, did you know Luparello?'

'I knew who he was. Rizzo's always been Giacomo's lawyer. And I don't know a bloody thing about politics.' She stretched, arching her arms behind her head. 'I'm getting bored. Too bad. I thought an encounter with a cop would be more exciting. Could you tell me where we're going? Is there still far to go?'

'We're almost there.'

*

After they passed the San Filippo bend, the woman grew nervous, looking at the inspector two or three times out of the corner of her eye. She muttered, 'Look, there aren't any bars or cafés around here.'

'I know,' said Montalbano, and, slowing the car down, he reached for the leather bag that he had placed behind the seat Ingrid was in. 'I want you to see something.'

He put it on her lap. The woman looked at it and seemed truly surprised.

'How did you get this?'

'Is it yours?'

'Of course it's mine. It has my initials on it.'

When she saw that the two letters of the alphabet were missing, she became even more confused.

'They must have fallen off,' she said in a low voice, but she was unconvinced. She was losing her way in a labyrinth of questions without answer, and clearly something was beginning to trouble her now.

'Your initials are still there, you just can't see them because it's dark. Somebody tore them off, but their imprints are there in the leather.'

'But who tore them off? And why?'

A note of anxiety sounded in her voice. The inspector didn't answer. He knew perfectly well why they had done it: to make it look as if Ingrid had wanted to make the bag anonymous. When they came to the little dirt road that led to Capo Massaria,

Montalbano, who had accelerated as if intending to go straight, suddenly spun the wheel violently, turning onto the path. All at once, without a word, Ingrid threw open the car door, nimbly exited the moving vehicle, and started running through the trees. Cursing, the inspector braked, jumped out, and gave chase. After a few seconds he realized he would never catch her and stopped, undecided. At that exact moment he saw her fall. When he was beside her, Ingrid, who had been unable to get back up, interrupted her Swedish monologue, incomprehensible but clearly expressing fear and rage.

'Fuck off!' she said, and continued massaging her ankle.

'Get up, and no more bullshit.'

With effort, she obeyed and leaned against Montalbano, who remained motionless, not helping her.

*

The gate opened easily; it was the front door that put up resistance.

'Let me do it,' said Ingrid. She had followed him without making a move, as though resigned. But she had been preparing her plan of defence.

'You won't find anything inside, you know,' she said in the doorway, her tone defiant.

She turned on the light, confident, but when she looked inside and saw the video cassettes and the perfectly furnished room, she reacted with visible surprise, a wrinkle creasing her brow.

'They told me—'

She checked herself at once and fell silent, shrugging her shoulders. She eyed Montalbano, waiting for his next move.

'Into the bedroom,' said the inspector.

Ingrid opened her mouth, about to make an easy quip, but lost heart. Turning her back, she limped into the other room, turned on the light, and this time showed no surprise; she had expected it to be all in order. She sat down at the foot of the bed. Montalbano opened the left-hand door of the wardrobe.

'Do you know whose clothes these are?'

'They must belong to Silvio, to Mr Luparello.'

He opened the middle door.

'Are these wigs yours?'

'I've never worn a wig.'

When he opened the right-hand door, Ingrid closed her eyes.

'Look, that's not going to solve anything. Are these yours?'

'Yes, but—'

'But they weren't supposed to be there any more,' Montalbano finished her sentence.

Ingrid gave a start.

'How did you know? Who told you?'

'Nobody told me. I figured it out. I'm a cop, remember? Was the bag also in the wardrobe?'

Ingrid nodded yes.

'And the necklace you said you lost, where was that?'

'Inside the bag. I had to wear it once, then I came here and left it here.'

She paused a moment and looked the inspector long in the eye.

'What does this all mean?' she asked.

'Let's go back in the other room.'

*

Ingrid took a glass from the sideboard, half filled it with straight whisky, drank almost all of it in a single draft, then refilled it.

'You want any?'

Montalbano said no. He had sat down on the couch and was looking out at the sea. The light was dim enough to allow him to see beyond the glass. Ingrid came and sat down beside him.

'I've sat here looking at the sea in better times.'

She slid a little closer on the sofa and rested her head on the inspector's shoulder. He didn't move; he immediately understood that her gesture was not an attempt at seduction.

'Ingrid, remember what I told you in the car? That our conversation was an unofficial one?'

'Yes.'

'Now answer me truthfully. Those clothes in the wardrobe, did you bring them here yourself or were they put there?'

'I brought them myself. I thought I might need them.'

'Were you Luparello's mistress?'

'No.'

'No? You seem quite at home here.'

'I slept with Luparello only once, six months after arriving in Montelusa. But never again. He brought me here. But we did become friends, true friends, like I had never had before with a man, not even in my country. I could tell him anything, anything at all. If I got into trouble, he would manage to get me out of it, without asking any questions.'

'Are you trying to make me believe that the one time you were here you brought all those dresses, jeans, and panties, not to mention the bag and the necklace?'

Ingrid pulled away, irritated.

'I'm not trying to make you believe anything. I'm just telling you. After a while I asked Silvio if I could use this house now and then, and he said yes. He asked me only one thing: to be very discreet and never tell anyone who it belonged to.'

'And when you wanted to come, how did you know if the place was empty and available?'

'We had agreed on a code of telephone rings. I kept my word with Silvio. I used to bring only one man here, always the same one.'

She took a long sip, and sort of hunched her shoulders forward.

'A man who forced his way into my life two years ago. Because I – afterwards, I didn't want to anymore.'

'After what?'

'After the first time. I was afraid, of the whole situation. But he was . . . sort of blinded, sort of obsessed with me. Only physically, though. He would want to see me every day. Then, when I brought him here, he would jump all over me, turn violent, tear my clothes off. That was why I had those changes of clothes in the wardrobe.'

'Did this man know whose house this was?'

'I never told him, and he never asked. He's not jealous, you see, he just wants me. He never gets tired of being inside me. He's ready to take me at any moment.'

'I see. And for his part did Luparello know who you were bringing here?'

'Same thing – he didn't ask, and I didn't tell.'

Ingrid stood up.

'Couldn't we go somewhere else to talk? This place depresses me now. Are you married?'

'No,' said Montalbano, surprised.

'Let's go to your place.' She smiled cheerlessly. 'I told you it would end up this way, didn't I?'

THIRTEEN

Neither of them felt like talking, and fifteen minutes passed in silence. But once again the inspector surrendered to the cop in him. In fact, once they had reached the bridge that spanned the Canneto, he pulled up to the side, put on the brakes, and got out of the car, telling Ingrid to do the same. From the summit of the bridge Montalbano showed the woman the river's dry bed, which one could make out in the moonlight.

'See,' he said, 'the riverbed leads straight to the beach. It's on a steep incline and full of big rocks and stones. Think you could drive a car down there?'

'I don't know. It'd be different if it was daylight. But I could try, if you want me to.'

She stared at the inspector and smiled, her eyes half shut.

'You found out about me, eh? So what should I do?'

'Do it.'

'All right. You wait here.'

She got in the car and drove off. It took only a few seconds for the headlights to disappear from view.

'Well, that's that. She took me for a sucker,' said Montalbano, resigning himself.

As he was getting ready for the long walk back to Vigàta, he heard her return with the motor roaring.

'I think I can do it. Do you have a torch?'

'In the glove compartment.'

The woman knelt down, illuminated the car's underside, then stood back up.

'Got a handkerchief?'

Montalbano gave her one, and Ingrid used it to wrap her sore ankle tightly.

'Get in.'

Driving in reverse, she reached a dirt road that led from the provincial road to the area under the bridge.

'I'm going to give it a try, Inspector. Bear in mind that one of my feet isn't working. Fasten your seat belt. Should I drive fast?'

'Yes, but it's important that we get to the beach in one piece.'

Ingrid put the car in gear and took off like a shot. It was ten minutes of continuous, ferocious jolts. At one point Montalbano felt as if his head were dying to detach itself from the rest of his body and fly out of the window. Ingrid, however, was calm, determined, driving with her tongue sticking out between her lips. The inspector wanted to tell her not to do that – she might inadvertently bite it off.

When they had reached the beach, Ingrid asked, 'Did I pass the test?'

Her eyes glistened in the darkness. She was excited and pleased.

'Yes.'

'Let's do it again, going uphill this time.'

'You're insane! That's quite enough.'

She was right to call it a test except that it was a test that didn't solve anything. Ingrid was able to drive down that road easily, which was a point against her; on the other hand, when the inspector had asked her to do so, she had not seemed nervous, only surprised, and this was a point in her favour. But the fact that she hadn't broken anything on the car, how was he to interpret that? Negatively or positively?

'So, shall we do it again? Come on, this was the only time this evening I've had any fun.'

'No, I already said no.'

'All right, then you drive. I'm in too much pain.'

The inspector drove along the shore, confirming in his mind that the car was in working order. Nothing broken.

'You're really good, you know.'

'Well,' said Ingrid, assuming a serious, professional tone, 'anyone could drive down that stretch. The skill is in bringing the car through it in the same condition it started out in. Because afterwards you might find yourself on a paved road, not a beach like this, and you have to speed up to recover lost time. I don't know if that's clear.'

'Perfectly clear. Somebody who, for example, after driving down there, comes to the beach with broken suspension is somebody who doesn't know what he's doing.'

They arrived at the Pasture. Montalbano turned right.

'See that large bush? That's where Luparello was found.'

Ingrid said nothing and didn't even seem very curious. They drove down the path; not much was happening that evening. When they were beside the wall of the old factory, Montalbano said, 'This is where the woman who was with Luparello lost her necklace and threw the leather bag over the wall.'

'My bag?'

'Yes.'

'Well, it wasn't me,' Ingrid murmured, 'and I swear I don't understand a damned thing about any of this.'

*

When they got to Montalbano's house, Ingrid was unable to step out of the car, so the inspector had to wrap one arm around her waist while she leaned her weight against his shoulder. Once inside, the young woman dropped into the first chair that came within reach.

'Christ! Now it really hurts.'

'Go into the other room and take off your jeans so I can wrap it up for you.'

Ingrid stood up with a whimper and limped along, steadying herself against the furniture and walls.

Montalbano called headquarters. Fazio informed him that the petrol-station attendant had remembered everything and had precisely identified the man at the wheel, the one the assailants had tried to kill: Turi Gambardella, of the Cuffaro gang. QED.

'So Galluzzo went to Gambardella's house,' Fazio went on, 'but his wife said she hadn't seen him for two days.'

'I would have won the bet,' said the inspector.

'Why? You think I would have been stupid enough to make it?'

He heard the water running in the bath. Ingrid apparently belonged to that category of women who cannot resist the sight of a bathtub. He dialled Gegè's number, the one for his cell phone.

'Are you alone? Can you talk?'

'As for being alone, I'm alone. As for talking, that depends.'

'I just need a name from you. There's no risk to you in giving me this information, I promise. But I want a precise answer.'

'Whose name?'

Montalbano explained, and Gegè had no trouble giving him the name, and for good measure he even threw in a nickname.

*

Ingrid had lain down on the bed, wearing a large towel that covered very little of her.

'Sorry, but I can't stand up.'

Montalbano took a small tube of salve and a roll of gauze from a shelf in the bathroom.

'Give me your leg.'

When she moved, her minuscule panties peeped out and so did one breast, which looked as if it had been painted by a painter who understood women. The nipple seemed to be looking around, curious about the unfamiliar surroundings. Once again Montalbano understood that Ingrid had no seductive intentions, and he was grateful to her for it.

'You'll see, in a little while it'll feel better,' he said after spreading the salve on her ankle, which he then wrapped tightly in gauze. The whole time Ingrid did not take her eyes off him.

'Have you got any whisky? Let me have half a glass, no ice.'

It was as though they had known each other all their lives. After bringing her the whisky, Montalbano pulled up a chair and sat down beside the bed.

'You know something, Inspector?' said Ingrid, looking at him with green, sparkling eyes. 'You're the first real man I've met around here in five years.'

'Better than Luparello?'

'Yes.'

'Thanks. Now listen to my questions.'

'Fire away.'

As Montalbano was about to open his mouth, the doorbell rang. He wasn't expecting anyone and went in confusion to answer the door. There in the doorway was Anna, in civilian clothing, smiling at him.

'Surprise!'

She walked round him and into the house.

'Thanks for the enthusiasm,' she said. 'Where've you been all evening? At headquarters they said you were here, so I came, but it was all dark. I phoned five more times, to no avail. Then I finally saw the lights on.'

She eyed Montalbano, who hadn't opened his mouth.

'What's with you? Have you lost your voice? OK, listen—'

She fell silent. Past the bedroom door, which had been left open, she had caught a glimpse of Ingrid, half naked, glass in hand. First she turned pale, then blushed violently.

'Excuse me,' she whispered, rushing out of the house.

'Run after her!' Ingrid shouted to him. 'Explain everything! I'm going home.'

In a rage, Montalbano kicked the front door shut, making the wall shake as he heard Anna's car leave, burning rubber as furiously as he had just slammed the door.

'I don't have to explain a goddamn thing to her!'

'Should I go?' Ingrid had half risen from the bed, her breasts now triumphantly outside the towel.

'No, but cover yourself.'

'Sorry.'

Montalbano took off his jacket and shirt, stuck his head in the sink, and ran cold water over it for a while. Then he returned to his chair beside the bed.

'I want to know the real story of the necklace.'

'Well, last Monday, Giacomo, my husband, was

woken up by a phone call. I didn't catch much of it – I was too sleepy. He got dressed in a hurry and went out. He came back two hours later and asked me where the necklace was, since he hadn't seen it around the house for some time. I couldn't very well tell him it was inside the bag at Silvio's house. If he had asked to see it, I wouldn't have known what to answer. So I told him I'd lost it at least a year before and that I hadn't told him sooner because I was afraid he'd get angry. The necklace was worth a lot of money; it was a present he gave me in Sweden. Then Giacomo had me sign my name at the bottom of a blank sheet of paper. He said he needed it for the insurance.'

'So where did this story about the Pasture come from?'

'That happened later, when he came home for lunch. He explained to me that Rizzo, his lawyer, had told him the insurance company needed a more convincing story about how I lost the necklace and had suggested the story about the Pastor to him.'

'Pasture,' Montalbano patiently corrected her. The mispronunciation bothered him.

'Pasture, Pasture,' Ingrid repeated. 'Frankly, I didn't find that story very convincing either. It seemed screwy, made up. That's when Giacomo told me that everyone saw me as a whore, and so it would seem believable that I might get an idea like the one about having him take me to the Pasture.'

'I understand.'

'Well, I don't!'

'They were trying to frame you.'

'Frame me? What does that mean?'

'Look, Luparello died at the Pasture in the arms of a woman who persuaded him to go there, right?'

'Right.'

'Well, they want to make it look like you were that woman. The bag is yours, the necklace is yours, the clothes at Luparello's house are yours, you're capable of driving down the Canneto – I'm supposed to arrive at only one conclusion: that the woman is Ingrid Sjostrom.'

'Now I understand,' she said, falling silent, eyes staring at the glass in her hand. Then she roused herself. 'It's not possible.'

'What's not possible?'

'That Giacomo would go along with these people who want to . . . to frame me.'

'Maybe they forced him to go along with them.

Your husband's financial situation's not too good, you know.'

'He never talks to me about it, but I can see that. Still, I'm sure that if he did it, it wasn't for money.'

'I'm pretty sure of that myself.'

'Then why?'

'There must be another explanation, which could be that your husband was forced to get involved to save someone who is more important to him than you. Wait.'

He went into the other room, where there was a small desk covered with papers. He picked up the fax that Nicolò Zito had sent to him.

'But to save someone else from what?' Ingrid asked as soon as he returned. 'If Silvio died when he was making love, it's not anybody's fault. He wasn't killed.'

'To protect someone not from the law, Ingrid, but from a scandal.'

The young woman began reading the fax first with surprise, then with growing amusement; she laughed openly at the polo-club episode. But immediately afterwards she darkened, let the sheet fall on the bed, and leaned her head to one side.

'Was he, your father-in-law, the man you used to take to Luparello's pied-à-terre?'

Answering the question visibly cost Ingrid some effort.

'Yes. And I can see that people are talking about it, even though I did everything I could so they wouldn't. It's the worst thing that's happened to me the whole time I've been in Sicily.'

'You don't have to tell me the details.'

'But I want to explain that it wasn't me who started it. Two years ago my father-in-law was supposed to take part in a conference in Rome, and he invited Giacomo and me to join him. At the last minute my husband couldn't come, but he insisted on my going anyway, since I had never been to Rome. It all went well, except that the very first night my father-in-law entered my room. He seemed insane, so I went along with him just to calm him down, because he was yelling and threatening me. On the aeroplane, on the way back, he was crying at times, and he said it would never happen again. You know that we live in the same palazzo, right? Well, one afternoon when my husband was out and I was lying in bed, he came in again, like that night, trembling all over. And again I felt afraid;

the maid was in the kitchen . . . . The next day I told Giacomo I wanted to move out. He became upset, I became insistent, we quarrelled. I brought up the subject a few times after that, but he said no every time. He was right, in his opinion. Meanwhile my father-in-law kept at it – kissing me, touching me whenever he had the chance, even risking being seen by his wife or Giacomo. That was why I begged Silvio to let me use his house on occasion.'

'Does your husband have any suspicions?'

'I don't know, I've wondered myself. Sometimes it seems like he does, other times I'm convinced he doesn't.'

'One more question, Ingrid. When we got to Capo Massaria, as you were opening the door you told me I wouldn't find anything inside. And when you saw instead that everything was still there, just as it had always been, you were very surprised. Had someone assured you that everything had been taken out of Luparello's house?'

'Yes, Giacomo told me.'

'So your husband did know?'

'Wait, don't confuse me. When Giacomo told me what I was supposed to say in case I was questioned by the insurance people – that is, that I had been to the Pasture with him – I became worried about something else: that with Silvio dead, sooner or later someone would discover his little house, with my clothes, my bag, and everything else inside.'

'Who would have found them, in your opinion?'

'Well, I don't know, the police, his family . . . I told Giacomo everything, but I told him a lie. I didn't say anything about his father; I made him think I was going there with Silvio. That evening he told me everything was all right, that a friend of his would take care of it, and that if anyone discovered the little house, they would find only whitewashed walls inside. And I believed him. What's wrong?'

Montalbano was taken aback by the question.

'What do you mean, what's wrong?'

'You keep touching the back of your neck.'

'Oh. It hurts. Must have happened when we drove down the Canneto. How's your ankle?'

'Better, thanks.'

Ingrid started laughing. She was changing moods from one moment to the next, like a child.

'What's so funny?'

'Your neck, my ankle – we're like two hospital patients.'

'Feel up to getting out of bed?'

'If it was up to me, I'd stay here till morning.'

'We've still got some things to do. Get dressed. Can you drive?'

FOURTEEN

Ingrid's red fillet-of-sole car was still parked in its spot by the Marinella Bar. Apparently it was judged too much trouble to steal; there weren't many like it in Montelusa and its environs.

'Take your car and follow me,' said Montalbano. 'We're going back to Capo Massaria.'

'Oh, God! To do what?' Ingrid pouted. She really didn't feel like it, and the inspector realized this.

'It's in your own interests.'

*

By the glare of the headlights, which he quickly turned off, Montalbano realized that the entrance gate to the house was open. He got out and walked over to Ingrid's car.

'Wait for me here. Turn off your headlights. Do

you remember whether we closed the gate when we left?'

'I don't really remember, but I'm pretty sure we did.'

'Turn your car round and make as little noise as possible.'

She did as he said and the car's nose pointed toward the main road.

'Now listen to what I say. I'm going down there. You keep your ears pricked, and if you hear me shout or notice anything suspicious, don't think twice, just push off and go home.'

'Do you think there's someone inside?'

'I don't know. Just do as I said.'

From his car he took the bag and his pistol. He headed off, trying to step as lightly as possible, and descended the staircase. This time the front door opened without any resistance or sound. He passed through the doorway, pistol in hand. The large room was somehow dimly illuminated by reflections off the water. He kicked open the bathroom door and then the others one by one, feeling ridiculously like the hero of an American TV programme. There was nobody in the house, nor was there any sign that anyone else had been there. It didn't take much to convince him that he himself had left the gate open. He slid open the picture window and looked below. At that point Capo Massaria jutted out over the sea like a ship's prow. The water below must have been quite deep. He ballasted Ingrid's bag with some silverware and a heavy crystal ashtray, spun it around over his head and hurled it out to sea. It wouldn't be so easily found again. Then he took everything that belonged to Ingrid from the wardrobe in the bedroom and went outside, making sure the front door was well shut. As soon as he appeared at the top of the stairs, he was bathed in the glare of Ingrid's headlights.

'I told you to keep your lights *off*. And why did you turn the car back around?'

'I didn't want to leave you here alone. If there was trouble . . .'

'Here are your clothes.'

She took them and put them on the passenger seat.

'Where's the bag?'

'I threw it into the sea. Now go back home. They have nothing left to frame you with.'

Ingrid got out of the car, walked up to Montalbano, and embraced him. She stayed that way awhile, her head leaning on his chest. Then, without looking back at him, she got back into her car, put it in gear, and left.

*

Right at the entrance to the bridge over the Canneto a car was stopped, blocking most of the road. A man was standing there, elbows propped against the roof of the car, hands covering his face, lightly rocking back and forth.

'Anything wrong?' asked Montalbano, pulling up.

The man turned round. His face was covered with blood, which poured out of a broad gash in the middle of his forehead.

'Some bastard,' he said.

'I don't understand. Please explain.' Montalbano got out of the car and approached him.

'I was breezing quietly along when this son of a bitch passes me, practically running me off the road. So I got pissed off and started chasing after him, honking the horn and flashing my lights. Suddenly the guy puts on his brakes and turns the car sideways. He gets out of the car, and he's got something in his hand that I can't make out, and I get scared, thinking he's got a weapon. He comes toward me – my window was down – and without saying a word he bashes me with that thing, which I realized was a monkey wrench.'

'Do you need assistance?'

'No, I think the bleeding's gonna stop.'

'Do you want to file a police report?'

'Don't make me laugh. My head hurts.'

'Do you want me to take you to the hospital?'

'Would you please mind your own fucking business?'

*

How long had it been since he'd had a proper night of God-given sleep? Now he had this bloody pain at the back of his head that wouldn't give him a moment's peace. It continued unabated, and even if he lay still, belly up or belly down, it made no difference, the pain persisted, silent, insidious, without any sharp pangs, which possibly made it worse. He turned on the light. It was four o'clock. On the bedside table were still the salve and roll of gauze he'd used on Ingrid. He grabbed them and, in front of the bathroom mirror, rubbed a little of the salve on the nape of his neck – maybe it would give him some relief – then wrapped his neck in the gauze, securing it with a piece of adhesive tape. But perhaps he put the wrap on too tight; he had trouble moving his head. He looked at himself in the mirror, and at that moment a blinding flash exploded in his brain, drowning out even the bathroom light. He felt like a comic-book character with X-ray vision who could see all the way inside of things.

In grammar school he'd had an old priest as his teacher of religion. 'Truth is light,' the priest had said one day.

Montalbano, never very studious, had been a mischievous pupil, always sitting in the last row.

'So that must mean that if everyone in the family tells the truth, they save on the electric bill.'

He had made this comment aloud which had got him kicked out of the classroom.

Now, some thirty-odd years after the fact, he silently asked the old priest to forgive him.

*

'Boy, do you look ugly today!' exclaimed Fazio as soon as he saw the inspector come in to work. 'Not feeling well?'

'Leave me alone,' was Montalbano's reply. 'Any news of Gambardella? Did you find him?'

'Nothing. Vanished. I've decided we'll end up finding him back in the woods somewhere, eaten by dogs.'

There was something, however, in the sergeant's tone of voice that he found suspicious; he had known him for too many years.

'Anything wrong?'

'It's Gallo. He's gone to the emergency room. Hurt his arm. Nothing serious.'

'How'd it happen?'

'With the squad car.'

'Did he crash it speeding?'

'Yes.'

'Are you going to spit it out or do you need a midwife to pull the words out of your mouth?'

'Well, I'd sent him to the town market on an emergency, some kind of brawl, and he took off in a hurry – you know how he is – and he skidded and crashed into a telephone pole. The car got towed to our depot in Montelusa and they gave us another.'

'Tell me the truth, Fazio: had the tyres been slashed?'

'Yes.'

'And did Gallo check, as I had told him a hundred times to do? Can't you clowns understand that slashing tyres is the national sport in this goddamned country? Tell him he'd better not show his face at the office or I'll bust his arse.'

He slammed the door to his room, furious. Searching inside a tin can in which he kept almost everything from postage stamps to buttons, he found the key to the old factory and went out without saying goodbye.

*

Sitting on the rotten beam near where he'd found Ingrid's bag, he was staring at what had previously looked like an unidentifiable object, a kind of coupling sleeve for pipes, but which he now easily identified: it was a neck brace, brand-new, though it had clearly been used. As if by power of suggestion, his neck started hurting again. He got up, grabbed the brace, left the old factory, and returned to headquarters.

*

'Inspector? This is Stefano Luparello.'

'What can I do for you?'

'Yesterday I told my cousin Giorgio you wanted to see him this morning at ten. Just ten minutes ago, however, my aunt, Giorgio's mother, called me. I don't think Giorgio can come to see you, though he had intended to do so.'

'What happened?'

'I'm not exactly sure, but apparently he was out all night, my aunt said. He got back just a little while ago, around nine o'clock, in a pitiful state.'

'Excuse me, Mr Luparello, but I believe your mother told me he sleeps at your house.'

'He did, but only until my father died, then he moved back home. At our house, without Father around, he felt uneasy. Anyway, my aunt called the doctor, who gave him a shot of sedative. He's in a deep sleep right now. I'm very sorry for him, you know. He was probably too attached to Father.'

'I understand. But if you see your cousin, tell him I really do need to talk to him. No hurry, though, nothing important, at his convenience.'

'Of course. Ah, Mama, who's right next to me, tells me to give you her regards.'

'And I send mine. Tell her I – Your mother is an

extraordinary woman, Mr Luparello. Tell her I respect her immensely.'

'I certainly shall, thank you.'

*

Montalbano spent one hour signing papers and a few more hours writing. They were complicated and useless questionnaires for the public prosecutor's office. Suddenly Galluzzo, without knocking, threw open the door with such violence that it crashed against the wall. He was clearly upset.

'What the fuck! What is it?'

'Montelusa headquarters just called. Counsellor Rizzo's been murdered. Shot. They found him next to his car, in the San Giusippuzzu district. If you want, I'll find out more.'

'Forget it, I'm going there myself.'

Montalbano looked at his watch – eleven o'clock – and rushed out of the door.

*

Nobody answered at Saro's flat. Montalbano knocked at the next-door apartment, and a little old lady with a belligerent face opened up.

'What is it? What you doin', botherin' people like this?' she said in thick dialect.

'Excuse me, signora, I was looking for Mr and Mrs Montaperto.'

'The mister and the missus! Some mister and missus! Them's garbage people. Scum!'

Relations apparently were not good between the two families.

'And who are you?'

'I'm a police inspector.'

The woman's face lit up, and she started yelling in a tone of extreme contentedness.

'Turiddru! Turiddru! Come here, quick!'

'What is it?' asked a very skinny old man, appearing.

'This man's a police inspector! Doncha see I was right! D'ya see who the cops are lookin' for? D'ya see they were nasty folk! D'ya see they ran away so they wouldn't end up in jail?'

'When did they leave, signora?'

'Not half an hour ago. With the li'l brat. You go after 'em right now, you might still catch 'em along the road.'

'Thank you, signora. I'm going after them right now.'

Saro, his wife, and their little son had made it.

*

Along the road to Montelusa the inspector was stopped twice, first by an army patrol of Alpinists and then by another patrol of carabinieri. The worst came on the way to San Giusippuzzu, where between barricades and checkpoints it took him forty-five minutes to go less than three miles. At the scene he found the commissioner, the colonel of the carabinieri, and the entire Montelusa police department on a full day. Even Anna was there, though she pretended not to see him. Jacomuzzi was looking around, trying to find someone to tell him the whole story in minute detail. As soon as he saw Montalbano, he came running up to him.

'A textbook execution, utterly ruthless.'

'How many were there?'

'Just one, or at least only one fired the gun. The poor counsellor left his study at six-thirty this morning. He'd picked up some documents and headed toward Tabbìta, where he had an appointment with a client. He left the study alone – this much is certain – but along the way he picked up someone he knew in the car.'

'Maybe it was someone who thumbed a ride.'

Jacomuzzi burst into laughter so loud that a few people nearby turned and stared at him. 'Can you picture Rizzo, with all the responsibilities he has on his shoulders, blithely giving a ride to a total stranger? The guy had to beware of his own shadow! You know better than I that behind Luparello there was Rizzo. No, no, it was definitely someone he knew, a Mafioso.'

'A Mafioso, you think?'

'I'd bet my life on it. The Mafia raised the price – they always ask for more – and the politicians aren't always in a position to satisfy their demands. But there's another hypothesis. He may have made a mistake, now that he felt stronger after his recent appointment. And they made him pay for it.'

'Jacomuzzi, my congratulations, this morning you're particularly lucid – apparently you had a good shit. How can you be so sure of what you're saying?'

'By the way the guy killed him. First he kicked him in the balls, then had him kneel down, placed his gun against the back of his neck, and fired.'

Immediately a pang shot through Montalbano's neck.

'What kind of gun?'

'Pasquano says that at a glance, considering the entrance and exit wounds and the fact that the barrel was practically pressed against his skin, it must have been a 7.65.'

'Inspector Montalbano!'

'The commissioner's calling you,' said Jacomuzzi, and he stole away.

The commissioner held his hand out to Montalbano, and they exchanged smiles.

'What are you doing here?'

'Actually, Mr Commissioner, I was just leaving. I happened to be in Montelusa when I heard the news, and I came out of curiosity, pure and simple.'

'See you this evening, then. Don't forget! My wife is expecting you.'

*

It was a conjecture, only a conjecture, and so fragile that if he had stopped a moment to consider it well, it would have quickly evaporated. And yet he kept the accelerator pressed to the floor and even risked being shot at as he drove through a roadblock. When he got to Capo Massaria, he bolted out of the car without even bothering to turn off the engine, leaving the door wide open, easily opened the gate and the front door of the house, and raced into the bedroom. The pistol in the drawer of the bedside table was gone. He cursed himself violently. He'd been an idiot: after discovering the weapon on his first visit, he had been back to the house twice with Ingrid and hadn't bothered to check if the gun was still in its place, not once, not even when he'd found the gate open and had set his own mind at rest, convinced that it was he who'd forgotten to shut it.

*

And now I'm going to dawdle a bit, he thought as soon as he got home. He liked the verb 'dawdle', *tambasiare* in Sicilian, which meant poking about from room to room without a precise goal, preferably doing pointless things. Which he did: he rearranged his books, put his desk in order, straightened a drawing on the wall, cleaned the gas burners on the stove. He was dawdling. He had no appetite, had not gone to the restaurant, hadn't even opened the refrigerator to see what Adelina had prepared for him.

Upon entering, he had as usual turned on the television. The first item on the Televigàta news gave the details surrounding the murder of Counsellor Rizzo. Only the details, because the initial announcement of the event had already been given in an emergency broadcast. The newsman had no doubt about it, Rizzo had been ruthlessly murdered by the Mafia, which became frightened when the deceased had recently risen to a position of great political responsibility from which he could better carry on the struggle against organized crime. For this was the watchword of the political renewal: all-out war against the Mafia. Even Nicolò Zito, having rushed back from Palermo, spoke of the Mafia on the Free Channel, but he did so in such contorted fashion that it was impossible to understand anything he said. Between the lines – indeed, between the words – Montalbano sensed that Zito thought it had actually been a brutal settling of scores but wouldn't say so openly, fearing yet another lawsuit among the hundreds he already had pending against him. Finally Montalbano got tired of all the empty chatter, turned off the television, closed the shutters to keep the daylight out, threw himself down on the bed, still dressed, and curled up. What he wanted to do now was *accuttufarsi* – another verb he liked, which meant at once to be beaten up and to withdraw from human society. At that moment, for Montalbano, both meanings were more than applicable.

FIFTEEN

More than a new recipe for baby octopus, the dish invented by Signora Elisa, the commissioner's wife, seemed to Montalbano's palate a truly divine inspiration. He served himself an abundant second helping, but when he saw that this one, too, was coming to an end, he slowed down the rhythm of his chewing, to prolong, however briefly, the pleasure that delicacy afforded him. Signora Elisa watched him happily; like all good cooks, she took delight in the expressions that formed on the faces of her table companions as they tasted one of her creations. And Montalbano, because he had such an expressive face, was one of her favourite dinner guests.

'Thank you very, very much,' the inspector said to her at the end of the meal, sighing. The *purpiteddri* had worked a sort of partial miracle – partial because while it was true that Montalbano now felt at peace with man and God, it was also true that he still did not feel very pacified in his own regard.

When the meal was over, the signora cleared the table and understandingly put a bottle of Chivas on the table for the inspector and a bottle of bitters for her husband.

'I'll let you two talk about your murder victims, the real ones; I'm going into the living room to watch the pretend murders, which I prefer.'

It was a ritual they repeated at least twice a month. Montalbano was fond of the commissioner and his wife, and that fondness was amply repaid in kind by both. The commissioner was a refined, cultured, reserved man, almost a figure from another age.

They talked about the disastrous political situation, the unknown dangers the growing unemployment held in store for the country, the shaky, crumbling state of law and order. Then the commissioner asked a direct question.

'Can you tell me why you haven't yet closed the Luparello investigation? I got a worried phone call from Lo Bianco today.'

'Was he angry?'

'No, only worried, as I said. Perplexed, rather. He can't understand why you're dragging things out so much. And I can't either, to tell you the truth. Look, Montalbano, you know me and you know that I would never presume to pressure one of my officers to settle something one way or another.'

'Of course.'

'So if I'm here asking you this, it's out of personal curiosity, understood? I'm speaking to my friend Montalbano, mind you. To a friend whom I know to possess an intelligence, an acumen, and, most important, a courtesy in human relations quite rare nowadays.'

'Thank you, sir, I'll be honest with you. I think you deserve as much. What seemed suspicious to me from the start of the whole affair was the place where the body was found. It was inconsistent, blatantly inconsistent, with the personality and lifestyle of Luparello, a sensible, prudent, ambitious man. I asked myself: why did he do it? Why did he go all the way to the Pasture for a sexual encounter, putting his life and his public image in danger? I couldn't come up with an answer. You see, sir, it was as if, in all due proportion, the president of the Republic had died of a heart attack while dancing to rock music at a third-rate disco.'

The commissioner raised a hand to stop him.

'Your comparison doesn't really work,' he observed with a smile that wasn't a smile. 'We recently had a minister go wild on the dance floor of third- and worse-rate nightclubs, and he didn't die . . .'

The 'unfortunately' he was clearly about to add disappeared on the tip of his tongue.

'But the fact remains,' Montalbano insisted. 'And this first impression was abundantly confirmed for me by the engineer's widow.'

'So you've met her? Quite a mind, that lady.'

'It was she who sought me out, after you had spoken well of me. In our conversation yesterday she told me her husband had a pied-à-terre at Capo Massaria and gave me the keys. So what reason would he have to risk exposure at a place like the Pasture?'

'I have asked myself the same question.'

'Let us assume for a moment, for the sake of argument, that he did go there, that he let himself be talked into it by a woman with tremendous powers of persuasion. A woman not from the place, who took an absolutely impassable route to get him there. Bear in mind that it's the woman who's driving.'

'The road was impassable, you say?'

'Yes. And not only do I have exact testimony to back this up, but I also had my sergeant take that route, and I took it myself. So the car is actually driven down the dry bed of the Canneto, ruining the suspension. When it comes to a stop, almost inside a big shrub in the Pasture, the woman immediately mounts the man beside her, and they begin making love. And it is during this act that Luparello suffers the misfortune that kills him. The woman, however, does not scream, does not call for help. Cool as a cucumber, she walks slowly down the path that leads to the provincial road, gets into a car that has pulled up, and disappears.'

'It's all very strange, you're right. Did the woman ask for a ride?'

'Apparently not, and you've hit the nail on the head. And I have yet another testimony to this effect. The car that pulled up did so in a hurry, with its door actually open. In other words, the driver knew whom he was supposed to encounter and pick up without wasting any time.'

'Excuse me, Inspector, but did you get sworn statements for all these testimonies?'

'No, there wasn't any reason. You see, one thing is certain: Luparello died of natural causes. Officially speaking, I have no reason to be investigating.'

'Well, if things are as you say, there is, for example, the failure to assist a person in danger.'

'Do you agree with me that that's nonsense?'

'Yes.'

'Well, that's as far as I'd gone when Signora Luparello pointed out something very essential to me, that is, that her husband, when he died, had his underwear on backwards.'

'Wait a minute,' said the commissioner, 'let's slow down. How did the signora know that her husband's underwear was on backwards, if indeed it was? As far as I know, she wasn't there at the scene, and she wasn't present at the crime lab's examinations.'

Montalbano became worried. He had spoken impulsively, not realizing he had to avoid implicating Jacomuzzi, who he was sure had given the widow the photos. But there was no turning back.

'The signora got hold of the crime-lab photos. I don't know how.'

'I think I do,' said the commissioner, frowning.

'She examined them carefully with a magnifying glass and showed them to me. She was right.'

'And based on this detail she formed an opinion?'

'Of course. It's based on the assumption that although her husband, when getting dressed in the morning, might by chance have put them on backwards, inevitably over the course of the day he would have noticed, since he took diuretics and had to urinate frequently. Therefore, on the basis of this hypothesis, the signora believes that Luparello must have been caught in some sort of embarrassing situation, to say the least, at which point he was forced to put his clothes back on in a hurry and go to the Pasture, where – in the signora's opinion, of course – he was to be compromised in some irreparable way, so that he would have to retire from political life. But there's more.'

'Don't spare me any details.'

'The two street cleaners who found the body, before calling the police, felt duty-bound to inform Counsellor Rizzo, who they knew was Luparello's alter ego. Well, Rizzo not only showed no surprise, dismay, shock, alarm, or worry, he actually told the two to report the incident at once.'

'How do you know this? Had you tapped the phone line?' the commissioner asked, aghast.

'No, no phone taps. One of the street cleaners faithfully transcribed the brief exchange. He did it for reasons too complicated to go into here.'

'Was he contemplating blackmail?'

'No, he was contemplating the way a play is written. Believe me, he had no intention whatsoever of committing a crime. And this is where we come to the heart of the matter: Rizzo.'

'Wait a minute. I was determined to find a way this evening to scold you again. For wanting always to complicate simple matters. Surely you've read Sciascia's *Candida.* Do you remember that at a certain point the protagonist asserts that it is possible that things are almost always simple? I merely wanted to remind you of this.'

'Yes, but, you see, Candido says "almost always", he doesn't say "always". He allows for exceptions. And Luparello's case is one of those where things were set up to appear simple.'

'When in fact they are complicated?'

'Very complicated. And speaking of *Candida,* do you remember the subtitle?'

'Of course: *A Dream Dreamed in Sicily.*'

'Exactly, whereas we are dealing with a nightmare of sorts. Let me venture a hypothesis that will be very difficult to confirm now that Rizzo has been murdered. On Sunday evening, around seven, Luparello phones his wife to tell her he'll be home very late – he has an important political meeting. In fact, he goes to his little house on Capo Massaria for a lovers' tryst. And I'll tell you right away that any eventual investigation as to the person who was with Luparello would prove rather difficult, because the engineer was ambidextrous.'

'What do you mean? Where I come from, ambidextrous means someone can use both hands, right or left, without distinction.'

'In a less correct sense, it's also used to describe someone who goes with men as well as women, without distinction.'

Both very serious, they seemed like two professors compiling a new dictionary.

'What are you saying?' wondered the commissioner.

'It was Signora Luparello herself who intimated

this to me, and all too clearly. And she certainly had no interest in making things up, especially in this regard.'

'Did you go to the little house?'

'Yes. Cleaned up to perfection. Inside were a few of Luparello's belongings, nothing else.'

'Continue with your hypothesis.'

'During the sex act, or most probably right after, given the traces of semen that were recovered, Luparello dies. The woman who is with him—'

'Stop,' the commissioner ordered. 'How can you say with such assurance that it was a woman? You've just finished describing the engineer's rather broad sexual horizons.'

'I can say it because I'm certain of it. So, as soon as the woman realizes her lover is dead, she loses her head, she doesn't know what to do, she gets all upset, and she even loses the necklace she was wearing, but doesn't realize it. When she finally calms down, she sees that the only thing she can do is to phone Rizzo, Luparello's shadow man, and ask for help. Rizzo tells her to get out of the house at once and suggests that she leave the key somewhere so he can enter. He reassures her, saying he'll take care of everything;

nobody will ever know about the tryst that led to such a tragic end. Relieved, the woman steps out of the picture.'

'What do you mean, "steps out of the picture"? Wasn't it a woman who took Luparello to the Pasture?'

'Yes and no. Let me continue. Rizzo races to Capo Massaria and dresses the corpse in a big hurry. He intends to get him out of there and have him found somewhere less compromising. At this point, however, he sees the necklace on the floor and inside the wardrobe finds the clothes of the woman who just phoned him. And he realizes that this may just be his lucky day.'

'In what sense?'

'In the sense that he's now in a position to put everyone's back to the wall, political friends as well as enemies. He can become the top gun in the party. The woman who called him is Ingrid Sjostrom, the Swedish daughter-in-law of Dr Cardamone, Luparello's natural successor and a man who certainly will want to have nothing to do with Rizzo. Now, you see, a phone call is one thing, but proving that La Sjostrom was Luparello's mistress is something else. Besides, there's still more to be done. Rizzo knows that Luparello's party cronies are the ones who will pounce on his political inheritance, so in order to eliminate them he must make things such that they will be ashamed to wave Luparello's banner. For this to happen, the engineer must be utterly disgraced, dragged through the mud. He gets the brilliant idea of having the body found at the Pasture. And since she's already involved, why not make it look as though the woman who wanted to go to the Pasture with Luparello was Ingrid Sjostrom herself, who's a foreigner and certainly not nunnish in her habits, and who might have been seeking a kinky thrill? If the set-up works, Cardamone will be in Rizzo's hands. Rizzo phones his men, whom we know, without being able to prove it, to be underhanded butcher boys. One of these is Angelo Nicotra, a homosexual better known in their circles as Marilyn.'

'How were you able to learn even his name?'

'An informer told me, someone in whom I have absolute faith. In a way, we're friends.'

'You mean Gegè, your old schoolmate?' Montalbano eyed the commissioner, mouth agape. 'Why are you looking at me that way? I'm a cop, too. Go on.'

'When his men get there, Rizzo has Marilyn dress

up as a woman, has him put on the necklace, and tells him to take the body to the Pasture, but by way of an impassable route, actually by way of a dry riverbed.'

'To what end?'

'Further proof against La Sjostrom, who is a racing champion and knows how to travel a route like that.'

'Are you sure?'

'Yes. I was in the car with her when I had her drive down the riverbed.'

'Oh, God!' The commissioner groaned. 'You forced her to do that?'

'Not at all! She did it quite willingly.'

'But how many people have you dragged into this? Do you realize you're playing with dynamite?'

'It all goes up in smoke, believe me. So while his two men leave with the corpse, Rizzo, who has taken the keys Luparello had on him, returns to Montelusa and has no trouble getting his hands on documents belonging to Luparello and of greatest interest to him. Marilyn, meanwhile, executes to perfection the orders he's been given: he gets out of the car after going through the motions of sex, walks away, and, near an old, abandoned factory, hides the necklace behind a bush and throws the bag over the factory wall.'

'What bag are you talking about?'

'Ingrid Sjostrom's bag. It's even got her initials on it. Rizzo found it in the little house and decided to use it.'

'Explain to me how you arrived at these conclusions.'

'Rizzo, you see, is showing one card, the necklace, and hiding another, the bag. The discovery of the necklace, however it occurs, will prove that Ingrid was at the Pasture at the time of Luparello's death. If somebody happens to pocket the necklace and not say anything, he can still play the bag card. But he actually has a lucky break, in his opinion: the necklace is found by one of the sanitation men, who turned it in to me. Rizzo gives a plausible explanation for the discovery of the necklace, but in the meantime he has established the Sjostrom–Luparello–Pasture triangle of connection. It was I, on the other hand, who found the bag, based on the discrepancy between the two testimonies: the woman, when she got out of Luparello's car, was holding a bag that she no longer had when a car picked her up along the provincial road. Finally, to cut a long story short, Rizzo's two men return to the little house and put everything in order. At the first light of dawn, Rizzo phones Cardamone and begins playing his cards.'

'All right, fine, but he also begins playing with his life.'

'That's another matter, if that is indeed the case,' said Montalbano.

The commissioner gave him a look of alarm.

'What do you mean? What the hell are you thinking?'

'Quite simply that the only person who comes out of this story unscathed is Cardamone. Don't you think Rizzo's murder was providentially fortunate for him?'

The commissioner gave a start, and it wasn't clear whether he was speaking seriously or joking. 'Listen, Montalbano, don't get any more brilliant ideas. Leave Cardamone in peace. He's an honourable man who wouldn't hurt a fly!'

'I was just kidding, Commissioner. But allow me to ask, are there any new developments in the investigation?'

'What new developments would you expect? You know the kind of person Rizzo was. Out of every ten people he knew, respectable or otherwise, eight, respectable or otherwise, would have liked to see him dead. A veritable forest, my friend, a jungle of potential murderers, by their own hand or through intermediaries. I must say your story has a certain plausibility, but only for someone who knows what kind of stuff Rizzo was made of.'

He sipped a dram of bitters slowly.

'You certainly had me fascinated. What you've told me is an exercise of the highest intelligence; at moments you seemed like an acrobat on a tightrope, with no net underneath. Because, to be brutally frank, underneath your argument, there's nothing. You have no proof of anything you've said. It could all be interpreted in another way, and any good lawyer could pick apart your deductions without breaking sweat.'

'I know.'

'What do you intend to do?'

'Tomorrow morning I'm going to tell Lo Bianco that I've no objection if he wants to close the case.'

SIXTEEN

'Hello, Montalbano? It's Mimi Augello. Sorry to disturb you, but I called to reassure you. I've come back to home base. When are you leaving?'

'The flight from Palermo's at three, so I have to leave Vigàta around twelve-thirty, right after lunch.'

'Then we won't be seeing each other, since I think I have to stay a little late at the office. Any news?'

'Fazio will fill you in.'

'How long will you be gone?'

'Up to and including Thursday.'

'Have fun and get some rest. Fazio has your number in Genoa, doesn't he? If anything big comes up, I'll give you a ring.'

His assistant inspector, Mimi Augello, had returned punctually from his holidays, and thus Montalbano could now leave without problems. Augello was a capable person. Montalbano phoned Livia to tell her his time of arrival, and Livia, pleased by the news, said she would meet him at the airport.

When he got to the office, Fazio informed him that the workers from the salt factory, who had all been 'made mobile' – a pious euphemism for being fired – had occupied the train station. Their wives, by lying down on the tracks, were preventing all trains from passing. The carabinieri were already on the scene. Should they go down there, too?

'To do what?'

'I don't know, to give them a hand.'

'Give whom a hand?'

'What do you mean, Chief? The carabinieri, the forces of order, which would be us, until proved to the contrary.'

'If you're really dying to help somebody, help the ones occupying the station.'

'Chief, I've always suspected it: you're a communist.'

*

'Inspector? This is Stefano Luparello. Please excuse me. Has my cousin Giorgio been to see you?'

'No, I don't have any news.'

'We're very worried here at home. As soon as he recovered from his sedative, he went out and vanished again. Mama would like some advice: shouldn't we ask the police to conduct a search?'

'No. Please tell your mother I don't think that's necessary. Giorgio will turn up. Tell her not to worry.'

'In any case, if you hear any news, please let us know.'

'That will be very difficult, because I'm going away on holiday. I'll be back on Friday.'

*

The first three days spent with Livia at her house in Boccadasse made him forget Sicily almost entirely, thanks to a few nights of leaden, restorative sleep, with Livia in his arms. *Almost* entirely, though, because two or three times, by surprise, the smell, the speech, the things of his island picked him up and carried him weightless through the air, for a few seconds, back to Vigàta. And each time he was sure that Livia had noticed his momentary absence, his wavering, and she had looked at him without saying anything.

*

On Thursday evening he got an entirely unexpected phone call from Fazio.

'Nothing important, Chief. I just wanted to hear your voice and confirm that you'll be back tomorrow.'

Montalbano was well aware that relations between the sergeant and Augello were not the easiest.

'Do you need comforting? Has that mean Augello been spanking your little behind?'

'He criticizes everything I do.'

'Be patient, I'll be back tomorrow. Any news?'

'Yesterday they arrested the mayor and three town councillors for graft and accepting bribes.'

'They finally succeeded.'

'Yeah, but don't get your hopes too high, Chief. They're trying to copy the Milanese judges here, but Milan is very far away.'

'Anything else?'

'We found Gambardella, remember him? The guy who was shot at when he was trying to fill his tank? He wasn't laid out in the countryside, but goat-tied in the trunk of his own car, which was later set on fire and completely burnt up.'

'If it was completely burnt up, how did you know Gambardella was goat-tied?'

'They used metal wire, Chief.'

'See you tomorrow, Fazio.'

This time it wasn't the smell and speech of his island that sucked him back there but the stupidity, the ferocity, the horror.

*

After making love, Livia fell silent for a while, then took his hand.

'What's wrong? What did your sergeant tell you?'

'Nothing important, I assure you.'

'Then why are you suddenly so gloomy?' Montalbano felt confirmed in his conviction: if there was one person in all the world to whom he could sing the whole High Mass, it was Livia. To the commissioner he'd sung only half the Mass, skipping some parts. He sat up in bed, fluffed up the pillow. 'Listen.'

*

He told her about the Pasture, about Luparello, about the affection a nephew of his, Giorgio, had for him, about how at some point this affection turned (degenerated?) into love, into passion, about the final tryst in the bachelor pad at Capo Massaria, about

Luparello's death and how young Giorgio, driven mad by the fear of scandal – not for himself but for his uncle's image and memory – had dressed him back up as best he could, then dragged him to the car to drive him away and leave the body to be found somewhere else . . . He told her about Giorgio's despair when he realized that this fiction wouldn't work, that everyone would see he was carrying a dead man in the car, about how he got the idea to put the neck brace he'd been wearing until that very day – and which he still had in the car – on the corpse, about how he had tried to hide the brace with a piece of black cloth, how he became suddenly afraid he might have an epileptic fit, which he suffered from, about how he had phoned Rizzo – Montalbano explained to her who the lawyer was – and how Rizzo had realized that this death, with a few arrangements, could be his lucky break.

He told her about Ingrid, about her husband Giacomo, about Dr Cardamone, about the violence – he couldn't think of a better word – to which the doctor customarily resorted with his daughter-in-law ('That's disgusting,' Livia commented), about how

Rizzo had suspicions as to their relationship and tried to implicate Ingrid, getting Cardamone but not himself to swallow the bait; he told her about Marilyn and his accomplice, about the phantasmagorical ride in the car, about the horrific pantomime acted out inside the parked car at the Pasture (Livia: 'Excuse me a minute, I need a strong drink'). And when she returned, he told her still other sordid details – the necklace, the bag, the clothes – he told her about Giorgio's heartrending despair when he saw the photographs, having understood Rizzo's double betrayal, of him and of Luparello's memory, which he had wanted to save at all costs.

'Wait a minute,' said Livia. 'Is this Ingrid beautiful?'

'Very beautiful. And since I know exactly what you're thinking, I'll tell you even more: I destroyed all the false evidence against her.'

'That's not like you,' she said resentfully.

'I did even worse things, just listen. Rizzo, who now had Cardamone in the palm of his hand, achieved his political objective, but he made a mistake: he underestimated Giorgio's reaction. Giorgio's an extremely beautiful boy.'

'Oh, come on! Him, too!' said Livia, trying to make light.

'But with a very fragile personality,' the inspector continued. 'Riding the wave of his emotions, devastated, he ran to the house at Capo Massaria, grabbed Luparello's pistol, tracked down Rizzo, beat him to a pulp, and shot him at the base of the skull.'

'Did you arrest him?'

'No, I just said I did worse than destroy evidence. You see, my colleagues in Montelusa think – and the hypothesis is not just hot air – that Rizzo was killed by the Mafia. And I never told them what I thought the truth was.'

'Why not?'

Montalbano didn't answer, throwing his hands up in the air. Livia went into the bathroom, and the inspector heard the water running in the tub. A little later, after asking permission to enter, he found her in the full tub, her chin resting on her raised knees.

'Did you know there was a pistol in that house?'

'Yes.'

'And you left it there?'

'Yes.'

'So you gave yourself a promotion, eh?' asked Livia after a long silence. 'From inspector to god – a fourth-rate god, but still a god.'

*

After getting off the aeroplane, he headed straight for the airport café. He was in dire need of a real espresso after the vile, dark dishwater they had forced on him in flight. He heard someone calling him: it was Stefano Luparello.

'Where are you going, Mr Luparello, back to Milan?'

'Yes, back to work. I've been away too long. I'm also going to look for a larger apartment; as soon as I find one, my mother will come to live with me. I don't want to leave her alone.'

'That's a very good idea, even though she has her sister and nephew in Montelusa—'

The young man stiffened.

'So you don't know?'

'Don't know what?'

'Giorgio is dead.'

Montalbano put down his espresso; the shock had made him spill the coffee.

'How did that happen?'

'Do you remember, the day of your departure I called you to find out if you'd heard from him?'

'Of course.'

'The following morning he still hadn't returned, so I felt compelled to alert the police and the carabinieri. They conducted some extremely superficial searches – I'm sorry, perhaps they were too busy investigating Rizzo's murder. On Sunday afternoon a fisherman, from his boat, saw that a car had fallen onto the rocks, right below the San Filippo bend. Do you know the area? It's just before Capo Massaria.'

'Yes, I know the place.'

'Well, the fisherman rowed in the direction of the car, saw that there was a body in the driver's seat and raced off to report it.'

'Did they manage to establish the cause of the accident?'

'Yes. My cousin, as you know, from the moment Father died, lived in a state of almost constant derangement: too many tranquillizers, too many sedatives. Instead of taking the curve, he continued straight – he was going very fast at that moment – and crashed through the little guard wall. He never got over my father's death. He had a real passion for him. He loved him.'

He uttered the two words, 'passion' and 'love', in a firm, precise tone, as if to eliminate, with crisp outlines, any possible blurring of their meaning. The voice over the loudspeaker called for passengers taking the Milan flight.

As soon as he was outside the airport car park, where he had left his car, Montalbano pressed the accelerator to the floor. He didn't want to think about anything, only to concentrate on driving. After some sixty miles he stopped at the shore of an artificial lake, got out of the car, opened the trunk, took out the neck brace, threw it into the water and waited for it to sink. Only then did he smile. He had wanted to act like a god; what Livia said was true. But that fourth-rate god, in his first and, he hoped, last experience, had guessed right.

*

To reach Vigàta he had no choice but to pass in front of the Montelusa police headquarters, and it was at that exact moment that his car decided suddenly to die on him. He got out and was about to go to ask for help at the station when a policeman who knew him and had witnessed his useless manoeuvres approached him. The officer lifted up the bonnet, fiddled around a bit, then closed it.

'That should do it. But you ought to have it looked at.'

Montalbano got back in the car, turned on the ignition, then bent over to pick up some newspapers that had fallen to the floor. When he sat back up, Anna was leaning into the open window.

'Anna, how are you?'

The girl didn't answer; she simply glared at him.

'Well?'

'And you're supposed to be an honest man?'

Montalbano realized she was referring to the night when she saw Ingrid lying half naked on his bed.

'No, I'm not,' he said. 'But not for the reasons you think.'

Author's Note

I believe it essential to state that this story was not taken from the crime news and does not involve any real events. It is, in short, to be ascribed entirely to my imagination. But since in recent years reality has seemed bent on surpassing the imagination, if not entirely abolishing it, there may be a few unpleasant coincidences of name and situation. As we know, however, one cannot be held responsible for the whims of chance.

Notes

page 5 – ***face worthy of a Lombroso diagram*** – Cesare Lombroso (1836–1909) was an Italian physician and criminologist who theorized a relationship between criminal behaviour and certain physical traits and anomalies, maintaining that such characteristics were due in part to degeneration and atavism. Lombroso's theories were disproved in the early twentieth century by British researcher Charles Goring, who reported finding as many instances of Lombroso's criminal physical traits among English university students as among English convicts.

page 15 – ***The thought of going to the carabinieri . . . under the command of a Milanese lieutenant*** – The Italian carabinieri are a national police force, bureaucratically separate from local police forces and actually a function of the military (like the Guardia Civil in Spain and the Gendarmerie in France). Their officers are often not native to the regions they serve, and this geographic estrangement, coupled with the procedural separateness from the local police, has been known to create confusion in the execution of their duties. The carabinieri are frequently the butt of jokes, being commonly perceived as less than sharp-witted. This stereotype lurks wryly behind many of Inspector Montalbano's dealings with them.

page 18 – ***'phone the Montelusa department, have them send someone from the lab'*** – Montelusa, in Camilleri's imagined topography, is the capital of the province in which the smaller town of Vigàta is situated. In the Italian law-enforcement hierarchy, the *Questum* – the central police department of a major city or provincial capital – is at the top of the local chain of command and, as the procedural nucleus, has the forensic laboratory used by the police departments of the various satellite towns or, in the case of a large metropolis, of the various urban zones. The carabinieri use their own crime labs.

page 20 – ***'what's new in the chicken coop?'*** – The name 'Gallo' means 'rooster' in Italian, and Galluzzo is a diminutive of same.

page 30 – ***'Twenty million lire'*** – At the time of this novel's writing, about £9,000. Eleven thousand lire was worth about £5.

page 35 – ***Don Luigi Sturzo*** – Luigi Sturzo (1871–1959) was a priest and founder of the Partito Popolare Italiano, a reform-oriented, Catholic coalition that became the Christian Democratic Party after the Second World War. Persecuted by the Fascist regime, Don Luigi took refuge in the United States and never sought public office.

page 37 – ***Not even the earthquake unleashed . . . had touched him*** – This is a reference to what came to be known as *Operazione mani pulite* (Operation Clean Hands), a campaign, led in the early 1990s by a handful of Milanese investigating magistrates, to uproot the corruption endemic in the Italian political system. Their efforts helped to bring about the collapse of the Christian Democratic and Socialist parties but, as this and other such allusions in this novel indicate, the new code of ethics had trouble taking hold, especially in the south. Indeed the whole story of Luparello's career is typical of the Christian Democratic politician reconstituted to conform to the new political landscape while remaining essentially unreconstructed.

page 47 – ***'the prefect'*** – In Italy, the *prefetti* are representatives of the central government, assigned each to one province. They are part of the national, not local, bureaucracy.

page 97 – ***corso*** – A central, usually broad and commercially important, street in Italian cities and towns.

page 107 – ***the prince of Salina*** – Prince Fabrizio Corbera di Salina is the protagonist of Giuseppe Tomasi di Lampedusa's historical novel about Sicily at the time of the

Italian Wars of Unification, *Il Gattopardo (The Leopard)*. In a famous passage, it is actually the prince's nephew Tancredi who says, 'If we want things to stay as they are, things will have to change.'

page 124 – ***'Sicilchim'*** – The name of the abandoned chemical factory. It's shorthand for Sicilia Chimica, or Sicilian Chemicals.

page 169 – ***would jerk her head backwards, as if repeatedly saying no*** – In Sicily, this gesture expresses a negative response.

page 211 – ***an army patrol of Alpinists*** – The *Alpini* are a division of the Italian army trained in mountain warfare and tactics. Sporting quaint Tyrolean feathered caps as part of their uniform, their sudden appearance at this point in the story, though perfectly plausible and consistent with the government policy (mentioned on page 5) of dispatching army units to Sicily for the maintenance of order, is sort of a sight-gag, one that inevitably calls attention to the endlessly complicated and criss-crossing chains of command between the military and the local police forces in Italy.

page 236 – ***goat-tied*** – The Sicilian word is *incaprettato* (containing the word for goat, *capra)*, and it refers to a particularly cruel method of execution used by the Mafia, where the victim, face-down, has a rope (in this case, a wire) looped around his neck and then tied to his feet, which are raised behind his back as in hog-tying. Fatigue eventually forces him to lower his feet, strangling him in the process.

Notes compiled by Stephen Sartarelli